TWO PRETTY LIES

about this novel

Two Pretty Lies is a Hastings Brothers standalone, the third book in the series.

It contains plot spoilers for *Her Lovely Lies*. If you intend to read the full Hastings Brothers series, we recommend starting with the Twisted Beautiful Lies duet. The duet includes *Twisted Beautiful Lies* and *Her Lovely Lies.*

If you want a steamy one-and-done standalone, this book can absolutely be that for you as well.

also by kelleigh clare

HASTINGS BROTHERS NOVELS

Twisted Beautiful Lies (Duet book one)

Twisted Beautiful Lies: Extended Epilogue

Her Lovely Lies (Duet book two)

Two Pretty Lies (Standalone)

Two Pretty Lies: Extended Epilogue

SAVAGE SYNDICATE NOVELS

Wicked Rivals

Merciless Empire

Cruel Vows

For more info, visit

www.klclare.com.

TWO PRETTY LIES

HASTINGS BROTHERS

USA TODAY BESTSELLING AUTHOR

KELLEIGH CLARE

WHITE ROSE PRESS

www.klclare.com

Published by White Rose Press

www.whiterose.press

978-1-7355575-3-3

April 2022 Edition

Editors: Jovana Shirley

Cover design: © The Pretty Little Design Co.

Photo: © Wander Aguiar

For the readers who waited so patiently
for this little story.

It was not the thorn bending to the honeysuckles, but the honeysuckles embracing the thorn.

EMILY BRONTE

prologue

THOMAS

I STOOD WITH MY BROTHERS AT OUR FATHER'S GRAVESIDE, cursing at the old man while swearing to myself that it would be the last time.

Brisk air rushed in from the northeast and over the ridge, rolling across the estate and back out to the English Channel. The gust carried nuances of brine and evergreen and spring's wildflowers.

The wildflowers. Beautiful, resilient, and unintentional.

Like *her*—the someone. The one I planned to die for.

Death had never scared me.

As a child, I'd watched my father beat the fear of it out of my older brothers. From within the shadows cast by their giant forms, I had witnessed the repeated fracturing and mending of their spirits as he trained them to become his soldiers of fortune.

Richard Hastings had been the son of an earl, the next

man in line to inherit a title earned as spoils of another monarch's war. After a falling-out with the peerage, he abandoned the title. Still, his connections had remained strong.

Our father had supplied counterintel to Britain's military intelligence organization and conducted assassinations for Homeland Security. And because he was useful, the nation's ministers protected him. They overlooked the personal crimes he committed, the hits he made to line his own pockets, and the hits made for a protection pact that was part of our family history.

But while shielding him from prosecution, each of those ministers had also kept a personal running tab. My father's sins had accumulated like credit in their bank accounts.

On my eighteenth birthday, it had been my turn to become the next soldier in my father's legion. I accepted my fate without resistance, vowing to train hard and kill whenever it was necessary.

Three months later, my father had lost his life on a government mission, leaving the burden of his legacy and his debts on the shoulders of my three brothers and me.

After a decade of cleaning up our father's shit, only one debt remained for my family. But the obligation belonged to one of my brothers—to Will. I would reconcile this one myself to protect him, to protect his family, to atone for my emotional betrayal.

I dropped my gaze to the ground, where blue blossoms and ordinary woodland foliage fought for real estate.

Stepping between our younger brother, John, and me, Will gripped my shoulder. "Get in, find the information we're looking for, Thomas, and then get out. If your investigation proves our target committed espionage against the prime minister, detain him and turn the matter over to the director general. This is not a hit."

"I'll handle it," I said. "You have my word. Focus on your wife and children."

He'd recently learned that he and his wife, Ellie, were expecting twin babies. He'd also found out that he was the father of the eight-year-old girl we'd been led to believe was our niece.

Will's grip on my shoulder tightened. "Don't get drawn into the governor's politics, brother." Then, he gestured with his chin at the monument marking our father's grave. "Go on then. We're expected to have our arses at the breakfast table this morning before you leave for New York."

"Thom, if you need me, I'm not due back at university for quite a while."

"We'll see, John. Stay put for now."

Words on the granite slab grabbed my attention. The line below my father's name.

Beloved husband and father.

Empty space on the other side waited for my mother's death to fill it.

No way, I thought. *No fucking way.*

Anger overwhelmed me. It moved through my blood and filled my bones.

I glanced at Ethan's gravestone for a moment. We'd lost our oldest brother not long ago.

Eyes back to our father, I drew breath through my nose, pulling in another strong hit of evergreen and wildflowers, and stepped forward, closer to the stone.

Committing myself to the same promise that I'd once heard my brother make, I said to our father, "Listen, old man. When the time comes, my death won't be for the sake of your legacy. It won't be for you. I'll die for someone I love."

one

KATIE

I POPPED GRAPE NUMBER SEVEN INTO MY MOUTH, CRUSHING the skin with my teeth, and a burst of sweetness hit my tongue. A moan vibrated at the back of my throat. I closed my eyes.

It was a silly response to a small piece of fruit, but my senses were hyperaware after a weeklong stretch of only tea and oatmeal and isolation.

The number seven inspired waves of soft blue to flow through my mind, although the seven grapes that had been arranged next to my avocado toast were red. I wished for a moment that the server had put only six on my plate. Six was perfect. In fact, it was the smallest perfect number. A positive integer equal to the sum of its positive divisors.

According to Pythagoreanism, because six was an even number, it was also feminine. Maybe that was why it triggered flashes of vibrant pinks inside my head. For me, six conveyed vibrance and strength in all definitive formations.

Exhaling slowly, I opened my eyes, relieved to be out of the house.

It had been finals week, and those exams had brought an end to my first four years of college at Columbia University. In a few weeks, I would attend the commencement ceremony and celebrate achieving a bachelor's in mathematics summa cum laude.

Math came to me differently than it did to most people. Numbers were beautiful and colorful. I loved the ease of discovering new patterns, loved the fascinating overall structure of mathematics.

My parents, schoolteachers, and college professors called me a math prodigy. I couldn't remember a time when I hadn't been labeled that way. But the prodigy brand created a mask that I didn't like to wear. It concealed too much of me, hiding the things that made me a whole, feeling person.

I was more than a numeric expression.

I also loved flower gardening and taking photos and long afternoons spent wandering around the Metropolitan Museum's corridors, where photography exhibits by women artists provoked a feeling of power and satisfaction that resonated in my heart.

Academically speaking, in addition to math, I was interested in exploring the properties of modern theoretical physics.

No sooner had I dared to entertain the thought than two text messages from my mother's personal assistant hit my phone.

The governor is waiting at the apartment to see you.

Are you at the coffeehouse?

Of course, I already knew why my mother wanted to see me. Mom was in the city, and now that finals were over, she and my father wanted to discuss my extended future at Columbia. Their plan included a mathematics doctoral program, one in which I wasn't interested. It was a program that would leave me at the mercy of a boring university, teaching fellowship.

Still, always the good girl, I texted back with a compliant response.

Yes. I'll be right home.
Thanks.

All my life, my parents had sheltered me on the Upper East Side. My private school and the university were on the Upper West Side, so even when I was at school, I hadn't been far from home. I was only allowed to leave the city for weekends at the executive mansion in Albany or to spend time at our summer home in Southampton Village. I could visit the summer house either with my parents or with my aunts on my mother's side of the family.

While I loved New York, I still wanted out. I craved a better view of the world and a bigger role in it. London would be a good place to start, but the time didn't feel right to tell my parents about what I'd done and the opportunity waiting there for me.

My stomach growled, reminding me that I hadn't eaten my breakfast.

I started on the toast as I dug an envelope from Oxford University out of my bag.

The department head from the mathematical and theoretical physics graduate college at Oxford had sent a letter, inviting me to join the program. The university was offering me a fellowship. A fully funded package—tuition and stipend.

Jarring me from my thoughts, Jack, the coffeehouse owner, stopped at my table. "Hey, Katherine. Sorry, didn't mean to take you by surprise like that. I just wanted to say it's good to see you back this morning. Your exams went well?"

"Yes, really well. Thank you. I'm just happy to be done with it all. Your mashed avocado recipe is different. And delicious. What did you change?"

He smiled. "You noticed. Lime juice instead of lemon, a pinch of cilantro. No latte for you this morning?"

"I'll grab one on my way out. I need to get going. Mom's home."

The cashier called out to him, and he held up his finger to let her know he'd be right there. "I'll have one made ready. Coconut milk, lightly sweetened with brown sugar?"

I nodded. "Thanks, Jack."

The coffeehouse was a hip, cozy hangout, an art-friendly space with vintage furniture and rows of wooden tables. It was a popular place with considerable foot traffic. I spent a lot of time there, gathering with friends for breakfast before class.

At other times, it was a private escape for me, where I often devoured sweet lattes and the latest women's interest magazines from the corner newsstand. My mother had forbidden me from reading them at home, telling me the magazines were a distraction. Mom wouldn't know that many of them included more than a look at the latest style trends or dating advice. She'd never opened one to see the global coverage on women's health issues or international culture.

I watched Jack as he ducked behind the service counter, and I wondered what his last name was and why I'd never asked. He was a nice man, forty-two. He walked with a limp, but overall, his body was in great shape.

He'd served four tours in Afghanistan, and the stories he'd shared with me about his unit's hikes through the dystopian mazes of concrete blast walls were heart-wrenching. Starving children had lined the streets, patiently waiting every day in the hot sun for US soldiers to arrive with candy and bottled water. With their eyes, he'd said, they would plead for passage out of that hell.

Someday, when I called the shots, I would abandon this privileged life and use my God-given talent to help some of the world's broken children. So many lacked food, clean water, safe homes, and yes, basic math skills. I could teach them.

Completing my graduate studies abroad would be the first move in that direction.

My mother wouldn't easily accept the idea, not now, if ever. Dad would understand, but he still wouldn't pull his punches. He would say anything to stop me from leaving. He'd always been cautious about my personal safety, citing random threats sent to Mom's office as reason enough for his overprotective behavior whenever I questioned it.

I gripped the invitation from Oxford, pinching the three sheets of ivory stationery harder, the area around my fingernails turning white from the pressure.

I was sick of pleasing everyone else.

Attending Oxford's graduate program would get me one step closer to those children. And one step closer to having the world see me as something more than a math prodigy.

I smiled to myself, not even caring anymore about what my parents wanted. I knew what I wanted, who I wanted to be. I carefully placed the letter back into my bag, as if it were a golden ticket. It was exactly that, and it was mine.

The heat of someone's stare caught my attention. I

looked around the place, searching, stopping when I found the source. A man who I'd never seen before. He was twenty-eight years old, no less than twenty-seven, no more than twenty-nine.

He walked through the center of the room and sat at the table across from mine without turning his gaze away from me. His tall, well-muscled body moved with the refinement of a beautiful predator. Eyes ice blue. Fiery, not cold. They held mine, their strength compelling my cheeks to get warm, my heart to pound faster.

Influence and desire rushed through me. I was experiencing his emotions. Our locked eyes created a mutual, soul-stirring connection, and he used it to command me. I couldn't break free. I couldn't turn away from this man.

Then, as if we'd been playing a game that he had just won, he released me. A small smile touched his lips, and he winked.

I shivered.

His authority was hot as hell. *He* was hot as hell.

Every cell in my body warned me that this guy was dangerous.

Patterns of constants and variables and operations abruptly flashed through my mind, my brain acting on instinct to form and reform numerical expressions. Pushing math around inside my head was a reflexive behavior, a self-preservation mechanism that allowed me to regain my sense of self-control.

I took a deep breath.

Game not over.

Reclaiming my composure, I smiled back at him and then dropped my lids for a beat before locking my eyes on his again. I'd thrown a playful smile to flirt with an attractive guy in the past, but I'd never asserted interest with my eyes that way before.

The past didn't make sense to me in the moment. Being suggestive with this man felt right in the present. It felt good.

He was still affecting my thoughts and my behavior, I realized.

The idea of *all or nothing* hit me. He was projecting it.

Through his eyes, he insisted that in all situations, he would take control of everything, or he would have nothing at all.

There wasn't a thing in between his *all or nothing*, no other possibilities.

That was the danger I sensed.

My phone chimed with another text message, drawing me out of my curious fog. Desire for a stranger had consumed me, making me lose my way in a provocative haze, blocking my normal thoughts. The weightless sensation it left behind made me feel pretty and wanted.

The text-reminder alert chirped, urging me to look away from him.

I did but only because his phone started in as well.

It was my mother on mine.

Come home, Katherine. I miss you.

Dad and I are waiting.

I sighed.

Be right there, Mom.

She wouldn't have much time, as usual, and I missed her too. I fumbled with my things, cramming it all back into my bag. My smartphone fell onto the floor. As I dipped beneath the table to grab it, one of the baristas called out the to-go order for Chris. The latte Jack had ordered up for me.

For my father's peace of mind, I never used my own name for callouts in public places. I used his name.

Arriving at the counter, I shoved the phone into my shoulder bag and dug for my wallet while reaching out with my other hand to grab the drink.

Someone beat me to it.

"Oh, excuse me, but I think that one's mine," I said.

I looked up from my bag and found that ice-blue stare.

"Your name is Chris?" he asked.

"Yes. No. I mean, yes, it's mine."

The guy's larger-than-life presence was as stunning as his eyes.

He maintained his grip on the tall paper cup, his warm fingers fixed beneath mine. "Is it the name or the coffee that belongs to you, beautiful?" His voice made something in me quiver, the words offered in a polished British accent that gave him an automatic pass for the potentially offensive "beautiful" thing.

"The coffee is mine. The name doesn't matter," I said, twisting the cup in his hand to display the order label beneath the handwritten name. "See? Coconut milk with brown sugar. It belongs to me."

He smirked, his fingers brushing over the back of my hand as he let go of the cup. "It matters to me. I'd quite like to know your name now that we've established it's not Chris."

An odd sensation flashed through my stomach.

Numeric expressions. Breathe. Control.

"My name is Katie," I told him.

But that was a lie. No one had ever called me Katie, not once.

Somehow, the name had quickly found its way to my mouth and floated away from my lips like I had introduced myself that way hundreds of times before.

Like it was somehow the truth.

two

THOMAS

I FINISHED MY MORNING RUN EARLIER THAN USUAL, dropping out of the Central Park loop onto Fifth Avenue to meet my driver. He stood next to the car, holding a white towel draped over his arm.

Carl was an older man from the Bronx, a US veteran working beyond his service to keep food on his family's table, and he was one of the kindest people I'd met since arriving in New York.

A throng of nattering pedestrians shoved past him, causing his Yankees baseball cap to hit the ground.

I swallowed hard, my throat tight, the cords in my neck straining. My body was tense and my mood still dark despite the run. It wouldn't take much to rouse the anger idling at the bottom of my gut.

Anger was my constant companion, always waiting for someone or something to fuel it. Impulsive, heated reactions had always defined me, and curbing the instinct was hard as hell. I'd had to do some hard-hitting shit in my twenty-eight years, but I couldn't make excuses any longer. It was time to grow the fuck up.

Time to stop living in my brother's shadow.

Time to stop coveting all that he had.

His life.

His wife.

Time to move on and create a legacy of my own.

While touring apartments, I'd imagined how the energy and the opportunities that Manhattan offered would provide the distractions I needed to move forward. Three weeks in, and the constant noise and dense population only irritated me, making me long for the sprawling streets of London, where mainstream society was more introverted, more tolerable.

The truth was, I didn't want another meaningless distraction. I was tired of wandering the streets in search of shit that never satisfied me. I'd had my fill back in England, and it was foolish to pretend that more money and sleeping around in another country were the answers to my restlessness.

The craving tormenting me was deeper than that, more primal. The nameless desire upended everything in its path, pushing me to the edge of obsession, as it had done to my brother and our father.

I need to find her, the one who belongs to me.

The single-minded thought often consumed me. It was

a grim ballad, performing over and over in my head. But if you looked beyond the darkness framed by the words, it was straightforward and lovely.

She was out there somewhere, her name and the sight of her face withheld from me like some cruel joke. I dreamed that her eyes were perfect storms of innocence and longing. She would own me, the one with those eyes.

And I would ruin her. Choosing to be at my side, in my bed, living the rest of her life with a man like me would profoundly change her.

A group of men near my car abruptly grew quiet, their questioning glances drawing my attention. They parted as I walked through the center of their stupid fucking suit-and-tie collective and snatched up Carl's hat from the pavement.

I was glad for the anonymity in the moment, though it was only a matter of time.

Over the next few days, the details of a major leveraged buyout that I'd executed would become public, and people would stop wondering when they encountered me. Everyone in the Financial District as well as in the affluent neighborhoods would know my name.

Moving to New York had been personal for me, but it was also part of a strategic business plan for the global expansion of our London-based private equity company.

A decade earlier, my brothers had founded Hastings Group, sacrificing years to cultivate a family-owned business that was now worth billions. After our oldest brother,

Ethan's, recent death, I'd made my own substantial investment in the partnership stakes.

Will and I were starting up several new international operations, and I was more than pleased to conquer a slice of Wall Street's pie. More money in our pockets was certainly the objective. Money was power, and everyone wanted more power.

But the challenge of securing that power and the compulsive creative effort it required was what truly motivated me. And because we already had money, my brother stayed in the game for high-level connections and public influence.

Carl took his favorite ball cap from my hand and nodded to convey his gratitude, placing it back onto his head. He handed me the towel. "Coffee, sir? I know a shop just a few blocks east that has a smooth dark roast and a good breakfast menu. There're shirts in the storage compartment."

"Thanks, mate." After wiping the sweat from my neck and downing the rest of my water, I rotated my wrist to check the time. "Yeah, okay. There's a stretch before my first meeting this morning."

I pulled on a clean T-shirt and scrolled through email on my mobile phone as he circumnavigated the one-way streets to reach our destination.

He pulled up to the curb in front of Jack's Coffeehouse. "Enjoy your breakfast. It looks busy from the street, but there's plenty of space inside. Jack's a nice guy. Friend of mine from the service."

Six weeks before my arrival, I'd hired Carl to drive my executive car—a custom Escalade. He'd helped me find the car and supervised the vehicle conversion.

"Can I get you anything from inside?"

He raised the metal thermos he carried along each day and tapped on it. "The wife's special blend. Still hot. Thank you, sir."

I nodded, stuffed my wallet into my joggers, and popped out onto the pavement with *The Wall Street Journal* tucked under my arm.

A woman in her early thirties greeted me from behind the service counter after I pushed through the glass entry door and began reading the menu above her head. "Make yourself at home. Order here when you're ready," she said.

"I'm told your dark roast is quite good. I'll have a cup now, the soft scrambled plate—four eggs, four slices of buttered toast—and a takeaway cup, ready in twenty minutes."

She smiled as she wrote down the order. "Got it. What's your name? For the coffee to-go, I mean." She dispensed coffee into a ceramic mug and handed it to me. "How long will you be in town?"

It was obvious that I was an outsider. Not to mention, a foreigner.

"Chris," I snapped like a prick, giving her the shortened version of my middle name.

I pushed my credit card into the machine until it beeped and then found the nearest wall to put my back against while waiting for the food. I lifted my mug, blew at the steam, and drank while scanning the surroundings, one table at a time, until my eyes landed on a blonde sitting alone.

She held a letter in one hand and a slice of toast in the other.

She was beautiful.

I watched her. I couldn't stop. Her loveliness was rare and enchanting and painful. As I claimed the thick wooden table closest to hers, a pretty smile curved her lips. The weight of my stare alarmed her then because at last, she lifted her innocent gray eyes from the letter she was reading to search for me.

For a minute, nothing else existed.

In the following minutes, with our eyes locked, every goddamn thing existed. Base emotions raged inside me, and it had to be obvious, but she didn't turn away. She stayed with me, her wide eyes offering the obedience that I would demand if she were mine.

I won. She could be mine.

Ah, but this one was different. She deserved better than one night.

I smiled and gave a wink to disrupt the connection between us, to let her go.

Fuck if she didn't lower her lids and then hit me again

with those eyes, suggesting she wanted something more from me. She didn't want me to let go.

Christ, I wished she hadn't done that.

As if to save her from me, our mobiles announced messages at the same time.

I forced my attention away from the blonde. She wasn't the one. I couldn't allow myself to hurt someone like her.

It was getting late, my executive assistant's text message reminded me.

Good morning. Mr. Jensen in one
hour. Your office.

I seldom replied to Janie's text messages. She was able to see that I'd read them. She understood that if an urgent message went unread for an unacceptable amount of time, she should call me directly.

Checking my watch, I realized how quickly time had gotten away from me. I glanced once more at the pretty little reason for it, her eyes now focused on her own mobile phone.

A server set my plate in front of me. I crammed eggs and toast into my mouth, folded my unread copy of the *Journal*, leaving it behind for the next person, and headed for the counter to collect my coffee.

The barista had called out my name.

I reached for the tall paper cup while reading another incoming message from Janie.

Market update. 15 minutes before
the Jensen meeting. Your office.

Shit. I still needed to pop by my apartment for a shower.

Another hand—softer, smaller—reached for the same cup, closing round mine.

The blonde from the table.

She looked up from her bag, revealing those perfect eyes at close range.

"Your name is Chris?" I asked.

"Yes. No. I mean, yes, it's mine," she said.

"Is it the name or the coffee that belongs to you, beautiful?"

"The coffee is mine. The name doesn't matter." She rotated the cup in my hand. "See? Coconut milk with brown sugar. It belongs to me."

She was spirited, determined, and it triggered me, made me grin.

I released the cup but not without taking something from her first, brushing over her skin with the back side of my fingers. "It matters to me. I'd quite like to know your name now that we've established it's not Chris."

She hesitated. "My name is Katie."

"I'm Thomas." I gestured for her other hand.

"So, your name isn't Chris either?"

"Christopher is my middle name."

Katie nodded and offered me a sweet smile instead of

her hand. "Thomas Christopher. That's a really good name. It's nice to meet you, but I'm running late. See you around."

She was out the door before I could stop her. I hadn't been prepared for her to run out the way she did.

I should let her go.

It was too late. The compulsion driving me was stronger than my conscience. I followed her outside, calling out her name.

She kept walking.

I watched her, the swing of her hips enough to make me ache.

"Katie, wait," I shouted.

Katie didn't turn back. She disappeared into the foot traffic, leaving me stunned.

What the fuck?

No woman had ever walked away from me.

The barista stepped out onto the pavement with my coffee. "Here. You forgot yours," she said. "I recommend tomorrow's fair-trade Costa Rican. Stop by at the same time."

A smile flashed onto her face before she went back inside.

three

KATIE

My mother kissed my cheek as she prepared to leave, her time cut short by urgent matters of state, and I was relieved. It was her usual pattern. Home one morning, gone the next.

Patterns were simply a repeated arrangement in math, in life. They used to soothe me, but lately, so many of them irritated me.

I was relieved in this case because I didn't want to hear anything more about graduate school, and my mother was like a dog with a bone when it came to that. I needed time to think without being coerced. Oxford's invitation was still my secret, but there was an acceptance deadline. At some point, I would have to share the details.

"You have the summer to come around to it," Mom said, picking up her briefcase. I rolled my eyes, and she caught it. "Your point is well taken, Katherine. We understand that you're a young woman with desires of your own, but we do know best. Staying at Columbia for your PhD is the right thing to do. You're unique, darling. You must allow us to continue guiding you into your future."

"I'll consider it," I said to keep the peace.

Later, I would unpack my rebellious thoughts, transforming them into mathematical theorems. God, I was tired, exhausted by being "unique."

I wanted something more, to feel genuine passion and to express it in a way that ignited even more passion. I wanted to know what it was like to be outside of my small box.

But prodigies didn't behave that way—or so my mother always insisted.

"We'll continue to discuss. Don't forget to find a gown for the charity event, which is also the evening we're celebrating your birthday, and a dress for graduation."

"I'm sure I can come up with something."

"Get some new dresses, Katherine. I need to run now. Your father will be home tonight, and Marta is due any minute." Mom hurried into the elevator of our classic Park Avenue penthouse, waving good-bye as the doors closed her in.

Our fifteenth-story apartment was at the top of a prewar building owned by my father and filled with huge windows and French glass doors that led outside onto a wraparound terrace with open city views.

My father was a renowned architect who had designed

countless Manhattan high-rises, though he preferred the romantic structures, like the one in which we lived.

I turned away from the elevator doors and hurried to my room. I'd had breakfast with my mother, but I still planned to hit Jack's for a latte. Patterns and all that.

Standing before the mirror inside my walk-in closet, I took two steps back to catch the full length of my reflection, head to toe. I was taller than the average woman, standing five-eight with bare feet.

"He is much taller," I whispered.

Thomas Christopher. I couldn't stop thinking about him, his light-blue eyes and the way he'd looked at me. Leaving Jack's so quickly the day before without getting to know him had been a terrible mistake, I thought, one that I regretted.

It was unusual for someone to wander into Jack's and grab my complete attention like he had done. Or more like never. That had never happened to me before.

Pink lace on the adjacent shelf caught my eye. I chuckled and then slipped into the delicate bra and matching panties. My ripped jeans and soft chambray blouse concealed them, so no one would be wise to my little secret.

I wanted to feel pretty again.

"It was Thomas," I told my image in the mirror, saying his name aloud for the first time since meeting him at the coffeehouse. He was the one who had made me feel that way. "I think he saw me. The real me."

The elevator chimed.

Marta, our part-time and sometimes live-in housekeeper, called out to alert me, "It's me, Katherine. I'll be in the kitchen if you need anything, sweetheart."

Poking my head out of the closet to be sure she could hear me, I shouted, "When is Lena's last exam?"

There wasn't a day that I remembered when Marta wasn't part of our household. Her daughter, Lena, and I had grown up together, though we never attended the same schools. Lena was my best friend, the sibling my parents had never given me.

Whenever Marta stayed over to cover for my absent mother and father, Lena stayed as well, sleeping in the second bed in my room.

My bedroom was large enough for two queen-size beds. Dad had renovated the apartment several years earlier, merging two guest bedrooms to create a second suite for me. The point of the new layout was to give me a private bathroom and to provide me with a quiet study space, so I wouldn't be interrupted when he or my mother entertained.

Marta's bedroom was the third, located on the other side of the kitchen. Maids' rooms, as they had once been called, had attached bathrooms and were common in large prewar apartments like ours.

"It's today, right now. I'm sure Lena would love to stay here with you tonight. Your father will be late, you know," Marta said, now leaning against the frame of my open bedroom door.

I nodded and grabbed my bag. "I'll call her later. I'm hanging out at Jack's this morning if you need me for anything."

"It's raining hard, sweetheart. Grab an umbrella on your way out," she shouted at my back as I headed down the hallway.

May was often the rainiest month in Manhattan, and when I stepped outside beneath the large green awning, it was pouring, just as Marta had said.

Most of the time, even in the rain, I walked to the coffeehouse. But a bolt of lightning abruptly split the sky wide open, and the trailing clap of thunder rattled my bones and my nerves.

Some people enjoyed New York's late spring thunderstorms, but I loathed them. I disliked how the penthouse was exposed to the atmosphere and how my parents always seemed to be gone whenever the worst storms hit. The horrific ones, the ones where the city went dark.

My father's car was there, idling at the curb, and his driver, Walter, was drinking coffee with the door attendant. Walter didn't say a word. He gestured at the car with his chin and a smile.

I returned his smile and then fell into step with him beneath the umbrella he'd opened for me.

When we arrived at Jack's five minutes later, it was bursting at the seams with patrons, as was usually the case when heavy rain came down. Runners taking cover, businesspeople hoping for a break in the clouds, students cramming for their finals indoors rather than at the park.

There weren't any free tables or even any open seats in the back, none that I could see anyway, so after ordering my coconut milk latte to go, I waited near the red brick wall. I dug out my phone and scrolled through the social media feeds.

Family photos. Silly memes. Personal updates. Political posts. Unsolicited ads. Patterns. Numbers. Colors.

"Katie," he said, startling me, soothing me.

I'd assumed I would never see Thomas again.

His voice had been so close to my ear, so close. Goose bumps ran up my arms.

I made a mental note about how I adored his British pronunciation. *Kay-tee.*

I looked up at him, and he captured my breath, my words, with his shocking blue stare.

"Hi," was all that I managed to say.

"Hi," he repeated with a smile that lifted only half of his mouth. "Have coffee with me."

Four words, no ask, not really. I nodded. There was something about Thomas, something unspoken and elusive and commanding that was part of what made him so attractive. It was insane really. I was compelled to do what he wanted me to do.

"There are no tables available," I said.

"Come with me."

Thomas guided me to an area in the back, furnished

with worn leather chairs and a similar old sofa. I'd never used the space before. It was meant for relaxed conversations, but it always seemed to be occupied by young brainstorming entrepreneurs. Without a word, he angled his head, sending two guys in their mid-twenties away from the sofa to find another workspace nearby.

"Thanks, man," he said to them.

Did he know them? I had no idea, but it didn't matter. He was a man who was comfortable with taking whatever he wanted. Given his impressive size, I imagined the taking-of-things part was easy enough for him to accomplish.

Thomas turned to me. He was six foot four—it was my curse to know these things—and his shoulders were wider than any that I'd ever seen up close. He wore slim jeans with blown-out knees and a blush T-shirt that clung to his well-defined chest muscles and biceps.

In a soft pink shirt, he was the embodiment of complete masculinity. A small amount of ink was visible above the shirt's neckline, peeking up from his chest. More emerged from the bottom edge of his right sleeve. A serious urge to see those tattoos, to know what expressions he had characterized with them, overwhelmed me.

The beating of my heart and the sound of my breath rushed through my ears. A new sensation.

Adrenaline, I told myself.

I continued to stare at him, inspecting every inch of his face and his body while he did the same thing to me.

Dark blond hair. Long and thick on top, short sides.

He looked at his watch.

The watch—a modern Patek, like my father's—revealed that despite his informal clothing, he was a wealthy businessman of some type. With the relaxation of Wall Street's dress code, it was often hard to tell the difference between the newer generation on Wall Street and the guys at college.

"Do you have more time this morning?" he asked.

"Yes, I do. You?"

He nodded. "I'll grab our drinks from the counter." His blue eyes hardened a little. "Don't run out on me again, Katie."

The thought hadn't crossed my mind. I wanted to get to know him.

"I'm here," I countered.

Glad for an opportunity to pull myself together, I sat on the sofa and watched him walk through the center of the table-filled room and step in front of other people waiting at the service counter.

He was so damn confident, and I was so damn captivated by that confidence.

My phone was still in my hand, I realized. Lena wouldn't get her messages for a few hours, but I tapped out a quick text to her anyway.

Can you stay over tonight? Call when you get this.

Lena was good at testing the waters, dating men and women older than she was, and she would love the fact that I was opening myself up to talk to Thomas. God knew her advice wasn't always the best, but at least she was experienced in dating, which was more than one could say about me.

Reckless as she sometimes was, Lena was all that I had when it came to navigating matters of the heart.

I inhaled deeply and released the breath, wondering why Thomas had made it a point to come back today and have coffee with me. He was older than me, and he was the kind of man who could have anyone that he wanted. Why me?

One thing I did know was that his first impression of me had been different than it was for most people. I'd made sure of it. I loved the idea that he couldn't project the prodigy pretense onto me before I allowed him to do it. Of course, I planned to tell him because it would become obvious if we were going to have any real conversation at all.

I wanted that, wanted authentic conversation with him. But still, I wasn't going to show all my cards at once. Not this time. That never worked out well for me. Unloading the prodigy thing and the fact that I was the governor's daughter would change the way Thomas looked at me, as it had with everyone else who'd ever shown interest in me.

"So," I started, taking my cup from Thomas as he

returned and sat on the leather sofa beside me, "you're new here. Are you on business or visiting someone?"

He took a sip of his coffee and stared at me for a moment. "I would quite like to know you, Katie, so let's get our *curricula vitae* out of the way, yeah?"

All or nothing. There it was, quickly put on the table before me.

It was a bold move on his part—to demand we knock out the initial background information right away. Unable to stop myself from encouraging his bravado or accepting his winner-take-all position, I allowed my lips to curve into a small, approving smile.

He continued, "I'm from South East England, here on business, setting up an international office for the private equity firm that I own with my brother. I expect to travel between New York and London quite a lot. I'm an Oxford graduate with a master's in mathematical finance. I'm not married, not seeing anyone."

I should have known, should have seen his predisposition for numbers when he caught me up in his ice-colored eyes. People like him—people like us, we wore the identity on our soul, but somehow, I'd missed it with him. He would soon recognize it in me, if he hadn't already.

"I'm a New Yorker, born and raised, but I plan to travel. I'm graduating summa cum laude from Columbia University this month with a degree in mathematics. Columbia is expecting me for grad school, but another interesting offer has grabbed my attention," I said, watching his eyes drop to my mouth. Once, twice.

"And I'm not seeing anyone," I added in a more reserved manner.

Thomas stretched out his free hand and waited for me to offer mine.

Unlike the morning before, I gave it to him.

He held my fingers in his and caressed them with his thumb. "You forgot the part about how beautiful you are."

Something fiery shot through my abdomen, taking me by surprise, further undermining my courage. My face grew warm. I couldn't think of how to respond.

Where were the numeric expressions that should have been course-plotting through my head, giving my control back to me?

A small smile hit one side of his mouth again—an absolute panty-melting smirk. He was pleased with my flushed cheeks.

"I couldn't ask for anything more, Katie," he said.

four
THOMAS

BRICK AND MORTAR AND GLASS. A SMALL FRACTION OF THE dark morning sky. I could see nothing more from the window in my office. No bodies of water. None of the sweeping views of the capital that I'd been accustomed to in England.

The New York division of Hastings Group was quite a lot different from the conventionally designed headquarters located in the city of London. The company's home base was housed in my brother's majestic high-rise, where floor-to-ceiling windows provided our private offices with views of the iconic Tower Bridge reaching across the River Thames.

I'd leased space for a brief period in Manhattan's Financial District, allowing my staff to get to work while I researched investment properties closer to Wall Street. A permanent location with a goddamn view of something.

Beyond the elevators and the reception area, the minimalist loft we occupied had three private offices, a conference room, and a bullpen area that was furnished with tabletop workstations and casual seating.

Lightning abruptly pierced through the few gray clouds within my view, its reverberating thunder following within seconds.

I turned away to check the time.

Twenty-three hours and twelve minutes had passed since I'd set my eyes on Katie at that coffeehouse.

She had rushed out, and I'd followed her.

She never turned back, leaving me there on the pavement, calling out her name, thirsting for one more look, another word, the opportunity to touch her hand again.

I had thought about the connection we'd made every fucking minute from the time she'd first locked her eyes on to mine, flirting with her lashes, daring me to come closer. I hadn't slept more than an hour.

She isn't the one for me, I told myself. Same as I'd done throughout the night.

Katie was too pure, too good for me. I could see that.

The problem was, my impetuous nature was aligning with the hunger that lived in my soul, and the effect of that combination was stronger than my motivation to do the right thing.

I looked at my watch again. Twenty-three hours, fifteen minutes.

According to the barista's recommendation—her

obvious crack at providing me with cloaked information—Katie would be at Jack's again this morning in forty-five minutes.

"Mr. Hastings," Janie whispered, redirecting my attention to the business at hand.

We were ironing out final contract details for acquisitioning an underperforming publishing house in London on behalf of a global publishing company.

"Listen," I said to the four people on the telephone. "As I said, market share will quickly improve in the first phase of launch after we've capitalized on the neglected online platforms.

"Keep in mind that as narrow as the cash flow margin might be today, it remains positive. As for the final point of dispute, I'll discuss the assertion with Will and get his opinion as well. We'll reconvene this afternoon. No more delays, ladies and gentlemen. Takeover stays on the books for Monday. My team is more than competent and quite well prepared to assist you with a smooth transition."

Back to my watch. Forty-three minutes.

Janie checked my schedule on her tablet. "I'll reconnect everyone at two this afternoon. Please let your offices know to expect my call or email me your mobile numbers."

I watched her disconnect, make notes, organize her things.

Thirty-nine minutes.

The rhythm of my heart accelerated, each beat faster

than the last as it pursued the next, seconds running out the clock.

Thirty-eight.

Impulse surged through my blood and lanced my bones, driving me to do the very thing I had sworn I would not do. I should have fought the compulsion. I should have stayed in the office and called my brother to discuss that contract, but instead of doing the right thing, I surrendered to the urge.

Startling the hell out of Janie, I jumped out of my chair.

In that moment, I wanted to see Katie more than I needed air. My mind was stuck on her, and the conflicting thoughts that circled round in my brain demanded a resolution. Going to her was the only way to reconcile the variables.

Leaving my executive assistant there at my desk, I headed for the door, saying, "Find Jonathan Jackson and get him on the call this afternoon. His father doesn't have a grasp on the concept of technology or the advantages it will bring to the table. In fact, ring him now, and when you get him on the line, transfer the call to my mobile."

Outside, heavy rain assaulted everything in our path as Carl and I made our way from the building to the car under his useless black escorting umbrella.

"I didn't expect you so soon," he said, looking at me in the rearview mirror as he removed the soaked Yankees cap from his head. "Where're we headed, sir?"

"Coffee. Same as yesterday."

Carl nodded once, and his kind eyes smiled, as if we shared a secret.

I frowned. He'd watched Katie walk away from me.

"Might take half an hour to get Uptown with the morning rush and construction," he said, pulling away from the curb. "Should be towels in there with your shirts."

My mood was coming in too hot, and I needed to back it down. I tossed my mobile onto the seat beside me, dropped my face into my hands, and pulled in several deep breaths through my nose.

It occurred to me then. I was on my way to see a woman, and the usual rationale about how important it was to leave directly after fucking her hadn't even entered my mind—because I'd found someone that I wanted to know.

Twenty-nine.

As I looked round the car, my brain assessed the comfort level for Katie. I nodded, appreciating how the charcoal interior would suit her lovely gray eyes.

I'd purchased the custom-designed Escalade without a center partition, so it would be more like a normal car when I drove it myself.

Having the ability to keep working during peak traffic hours proved important, so my car was equipped with a military-spec mobile router that supplied high-speed internet and satellite services. A high-end television monitor lowered from the ceiling.

The custom interior had four electric bucket seats, finished in soft European leather. The rear seats reclined with power-driven leg extensions. I'd chosen not to have a rear-facing jump seat, using the space for my tall frame and storage.

Katie would be comfortable.

But I couldn't help thinking how amazing she would look, sitting next to me in my Maserati back home. Christ, the idea of having her alone in that car made my cock twitch.

My mobile phone rang, and it took a few seconds for me to switch gears and take the call, opting not to send it through the car's speaker system.

I pushed back into the leather seat and spoke to Jonathan Jackson, skipping a proper greeting and pointless small talk.

"Jax, you need to guide your old man to the other side of this buyout. He hinted at another potential delay. The subsequent cash loss a second delay would produce at this point in time is more than I'm willing to tolerate."

"He does want this company, Thomas. He knows it'll be an asset for our fiction imprints portfolio. I'll review the financials and tech gains with him before this afternoon's call. I assure you that once we sign, my father will step back, and I'll direct takeover operations on our end. I'm set to meet your team in London next week."

"Good to hear. Get it done, mate. And let me know later what you've put together for the ride this weekend."

"I know it was my turn to set it up, but I'm out on this

one. Last-minute change of plans. I'm flying to Las Vegas this evening," he said.

Jonathan "Jax" Jackson was an up-and-coming executive in the publishing industry as well as a friend.

We had introduced ourselves in the parking garage, where we both owned a flat with a view of the East River skyline. He commented on my Ducati one afternoon, mentioning he'd bought his first motorcycle the summer past.

We joked about buying sport cruisers for the freedom and the clear headspace that came along with riding and how, in contrast to that, we'd also chosen bikes with a passenger seat. Neither of us had anyone to fill the seats.

After a bottle of scotch one evening, he'd confessed he was screwed up over a woman who wouldn't give him a chance.

"So, you're following her," I said.

"Fuck you, Thom. You would do the same."

"Yeah, you might be right."

I looked at my watch. Eighteen minutes.

Quite right. I was doing the same thing, chasing down a woman who had turned away from me.

We disconnected, and my mind fell into its recurring trap.

The song. But it was changing, transforming into Katie's refrain.

I had been fooling myself for twenty-four restless

hours. I'd found something I wanted, and there was nothing to stop me from taking it, from taking her.

Some perceived the idea as strength, having the confidence to take whatever you wanted. But in truth, it was nothing more than weakness. A goddamn Hastings weakness, as my brother called it.

Carl made good time, getting on through the traffic, pulling up to the curb in front of the coffeehouse with a few minutes to spare.

He brought me back to attention with his baritone-pitched voice. "Sir, would you like me to walk you to the door with the umbrella?"

"I'll manage, Carl. Park and keep dry."

I stepped out of the car and into the rain.

The place was packed.

The barista who'd suggested I come back shouted at me over the heads of queued customers, "Large dark drip?"

I smiled in thanks for what she'd done and nodded, and then I turned round to scan the crowd.

There. Standing alone with her back against the same brick wall where I'd put mine the day before, her eyes set on her mobile screen.

Katie.

Christ, how I wanted to see her eyes again, to draw the weight of her unflinching innocence through them into myself and use it to wash away my past, to make me worthy.

As if the past even mattered at this point.

Pushing through the other patrons, shouldering the man standing beside her to make him slide over, I moved in close to her.

Her eyes were still focused on the screen.

"Katie," I said.

She looked up at me with one breathless little word.

I smiled. Her lovely gray stare was mine now.

"Hi," I repeated back to her.

A light blush spread over her cheeks, and the desire to worship her struck me, my chest aching with it—something I'd never experienced with another woman.

My erection came to attention then, reshaping the one fleeting moment when my yearning had consisted of something good and pure, turning it into selfish desire.

But she agreed to sit with me, no questions asked.

Leading Katie to the far end of the shop with my hand on the small of her back, asserting an undeserved claim, I cleared a casual seating area.

I had decided to stay at the coffeehouse with her, though it would've been quite easy to convince her to leave with me. Jack's was familiar to her and relaxed enough for me to explore whatever it was about her that I couldn't seem to shake.

"Don't run out on me again, Katie," I ordered, pushing harder into her gaze with mine, seeking and gaining her obedience before heading to the counter to fetch our coffees.

When I returned, she was unaware of the bloke

creeping round her, his eyes searching over her striking, refined features, his mind fantasizing about the things he wanted to do with her body.

Anger heated my blood.

Pride stirred in my chest. Fucking pride, as if Katie were mine.

"Get your arse away from her—now," I said, sending him back to his table.

Columbia University. Mathematics. Summa cum laude.

Katie's brain worked like mine. Numbers lived in her mind as vibrant, unsolicited expressions.

Her lips drew my eyes to them as she spoke. Their fullness was natural, the top as plump as the bottom. A mouthwatering pout.

Graduate school, she was saying.

She was young, an American Ivy League talent who had quite likely finished secondary school earlier than her peers. I assumed Katie was seven or eight years younger than me. The gap meant nothing as far as I was concerned. When it came down to it, age was an arbitrary standard in relationships, always had been.

"And I'm not seeing anyone," she said.

She was goddamn beautiful, and her scent was intoxicating. Soft and feminine but also untamed. Everything about this woman overwhelmed my senses. I needed to be closer, needed to touch her.

I didn't know what the fuck was wrong with me.

She's not the one for me. Don't ruin her.

Katie gave me her hand.

With her warm fingers relaxed on mine as I caressed them, I saw it then—that she could become my everything. There was nothing more than she was, and I told her so.

A pretty blush spread over her cheeks, as it had earlier, and then she dropped her lids for a moment before quickly bringing her eyes back to mine with a smile.

I smirked, pleased with her physical response to my touch, to my words.

"You'd like to travel," I said to lighten the moment. "Tell me where you want to go, what you want to see."

"Thomas, listen, I want to spend time with you," she said, pulling her hand away, her expression now serious, "and tell you those things. I do, but for that to happen, I need something you might not be willing to give me."

Concern switched on in my gut—a protective instinct. "Name it, Katie. As long as what you're asking of me won't harm you, it's yours. You have my word."

Her eyes burned into mine, the intensity and the depth of her longing cutting through the center of my chest like a knife.

"You said you want to know me. Can you get to know me without pressuring me for specifics about my family or my upbringing? I mean, if you agree to be patient, that you won't dig around or conduct research, and if this goes somewhere, I'll give you those details myself. I promise."

I nodded without a second thought. "Done. You won't be disappointed."

five

KATIE

Lying in bed, I stared at my phone, rereading Thomas's text messages from the day before. The first message caused butterflies to flit around in my stomach. The sensation shot up to my chest and then landed in my lower abdomen. I squeezed my thighs together to make it stop.

I'd given Thomas my phone number, and as we sat on the beat-up leather couch at the back of the coffeehouse, our knees accidentally touching on purpose, he texted me so that I would have his number as well.

"Read it later," he'd said, tapping out the words, dividing them into two messages.

> I'm quite sure this is going
> somewhere.

Let me know where to pick you up for dinner.

I waited to read the texts, as he'd asked, and then I never replied.

My mother had surprised me with a day trip back into the city. After that, I needed time to myself to think things through before responding to Thomas's confident words.

Later in the evening, he'd sent another. Reading it again now affected me the same as it had the night before. A shiver passed through me, and goose bumps rose on my arms.

Tell me where to find you.

I let the phone slide out of my hand and pulled the quilt up to my neck, folding my arms around myself beneath it.

Lena popped up from her bed and went to the French glass doors. "Why are you so cold? Look how the sun is washing out all the colors on the terrace."

"Do you need help, prepping for your interview?" I asked, ignoring her question. I wasn't feeling cold. I was feeling Thomas.

"Mama can help me get ready. If I get an internship at this fashion house, they'll probably have me making coffee runs anyway. You should text your guy back. Even better, you should call him. We decided last night that you're going to see him again, and I'm not letting you back out."

"I'm not backing out. I'll call, but not until after a shower and some caffeine. You know I'm hooked."

"Hooked on what, your expensive coffee drinks or the hot Brit who's definitely way into you?"

Tossing a pillow at her, I said, "Both, damn you. Go to your interview."

We giggled, and she grabbed her bag and left for home.

With Lena gone and after showering and dressing, I hit the elevator, passing my father as he was coming back from his regular morning workout.

"You look beautiful, Katherine. Are you going somewhere after Jack's?"

I shrugged, evading the question, and patted his shoulder. "Thanks, Dad. It's just an old sweater and some lip stain. See you this evening."

Though it was Saturday, my father would meet with clients or draft his latest ideas until late into the evening.

"Be careful, honey. You call me," he shouted at the metal doors as it abruptly closed me inside the box.

After a short walk, which had gone by in a blur, I arrived at the coffeehouse and ordered my usual latte, found a quiet table, and snatched up a copy of *Marie Claire* that someone had left behind.

Once settled, I drew some frothy coconut milk and espresso into my mouth and woke my phone. I bit into my bottom lip, staring at Thomas's text messages again without really reading them.

His words incited passion, the kind I'd been pining for.

Words, not numbers. Words made up of letters, letters that formed syllables, syllables that performed a different kind of methodical dance—one that now commanded me. Gave me courage.

Another sip. And another. My favorite magazine still unopened.

Smiling, I summoned the nerve to tap on his name and call him.

"Hi," I rushed out at the same time he said my name.

Kay-tee.

"Hi," I said again.

He chuckled. "I'm glad you called. I'd quite like to see you."

"My morning is open."

There was no reason to play hard to get. I'd already done that by not replying to his messages and ignoring his dinner invite, but also because my curious heart had decided to see him again the moment we parted after our coffee date.

Lena had said it was a date.

I added, "How about yours?"

"Open. Meet me outside."

"Wait, you're here … at Jack's?" I lifted my bottom out of the chair and looked through the shop's front window. I didn't see him. "Are you coming in?"

"I agreed to your terms. Don't keep me waiting."

Confidence rushed through me, filling my soul, his

commanding tone encouraging me further. He was keeping his word, sticking to my terms.

I was doing it—whatever *it* was.

"I'll be out in five."

"Good. See you in five," he said.

Not knowing where this day would take me, where I might find myself or for how long we would be together, I pulled in two more swallows from my latte cup and headed for the restroom.

When I stepped outside, the warm sunshine hit my face. Pedestrians filled the sidewalks, as usual, but moved at a casual pace, their sense of urgency gone for the weekend. The air temperature was ideal for the lightweight off-shoulder sweater that I wore with my jeans and cute leopard-print Vans.

I inspected the faces around me, the natives and the tourists moving in and out of the space surrounding me. I didn't see Thomas, but after scanning the curb, I found him waiting for me between two parked cars.

He stood next to a black motorcycle, wearing a sports-cut leather jacket that had likely been tailored for the width of his shoulders and a dark T-shirt beneath it. His blue eyes caught mine, and a brand-new thrill moved through me.

"Ride with me, Katie," he said.

Caught up in the moment, in his eyes, I nodded, though I'd never ridden on a motorcycle and I had no idea what to expect or even how to climb onto one.

Thomas grinned and reached for my hand. "Come here."

Slipping my hand into his, allowing him to pull me close, I confessed, "I've never ridden on one before. I don't know what to do."

"It doesn't matter. I'll take care of everything." His gaze moved over me, pausing on my bare shoulder for a minute. "You're beautiful, Katie."

"Thanks. That's really sweet."

My dad often said the same, but he was my father, and it was his job to say so.

I had never considered myself anything other than average at best. In the mirror, I saw boring, colorless eyes and lips that were much too large, like someone had just punched me in the mouth. And as puffy as my lips were, they hardly covered my two front teeth.

My face betrayed my thoughts, and Thomas leaned in with his chest.

"It's the truth," he said, his warmth filling the space between us.

Just this once, I wanted to lose my mind and feel nothing and feel everything. I wanted to touch his face, slide my hands to the back of his neck.

But I only looked up at him. Listening, waiting.

"We'll ride to Tryon. My car will be there as well, just in case."

Fort Tryon was a huge park set on a ridge in the northwest corner of Manhattan. It had amazing views of the

Hudson River. The wildflowers along the walking paths and the Heather Garden and the lawns were so gorgeous in the spring.

Tryon was also home to the Cloisters, a branch of the Met Museum and another place in Manhattan where I loved to spend my free time. Dad and I used to go together on our *skip out on real life* days, as he'd called them. While he had sketched, I'd photographed the flowers.

Smiling, I said, "Sounds nice. I'm all yours."

Thomas smiled with me, and then he let it drop, his face turning serious, his hand pushing through the underside of my hair to find the nape of my neck.

"I want to kiss you, Katie."

He didn't kiss me. It was an ask even if he hadn't framed it as a question.

While I stared into his eyes, considering his unpunctuated way of communicating, my brain busied itself beyond that. Not in the usual way, not with numeric expressions. Strange as it was, math was the last thing running through my mind. Being near him released me from that burden.

Instead of revisiting patterns and formulas, I thought about what I wanted from this man. He was older and further along in his life than I was with mine.

Still, I did want something. I wanted *more*.

My behavior was changing. I was growing selfish and imprudent after knowing Thomas for such a short time. But with him or for him, the means didn't matter.

"Take it from me, Thomas."

His fingers pressed into my neck, and he lowered his mouth close to mine. Only his words touched my lips. “Understand, sweetheart, I’m not the kind of man you want to tease.”

I wasn’t teasing him. In that moment, I wanted his kiss more than I wanted anything. A small voice inside my head told me to push my lips against his and take it from him. He was right there, so close.

A different voice stopped me, telling me that my first instinct was right. He was not only the kind of man who shouldn’t be teased, but also one who needed to own our first kiss. This kiss, it would be his way or not at all.

I lifted my hand and dragged my fingertips along his jawline, over the scruffiness of his unshaven chin, taking in another new sensation as it shot through my body.

“I want you to kiss me,” I whispered.

As Thomas held my neck, he ran his other hand along my rib cage to my bare shoulder, where he paused for a moment before taking my fingers away from his face to kiss them. A reward for touching him.

More than that, he was teaching me to give him physical consent, I realized. He’d picked up on my inexperience.

Thomas kept my hand inside his and rested them together against his chest, and then with our gazes still connected, our eyes still open, he kissed my lips.

My heart pounded faster, and my breath stopped. I

wanted to scream. I wanted to laugh out loud. God, I just wanted more.

Neither of us looked away.

"Katie," he said, a half-smile on his perfect lips, "you'll give me this day."

I nodded, allowing myself to get in deeper, throwing caution and well-behaved Katherine to the wind. "Today is yours," I said. "Show me how to ride with you."

He winked and turned to his motorcycle to grab a leather jacket that he'd draped over the seat, that damn smile staying on his face. The jacket was smaller than his, styled in the same sports-cut but more feminine. He held it in front of me, as if he wanted me to put my arms into the sleeves.

"It's for you." With a slight nod, he encouraged me to slip it on. "You'd be quite cold without one, and you need the protection. I have a helmet for you as well."

"Oh. Thanks. See? I wouldn't have known that. How did you know my size?"

I wanted to take the question back as quickly as it had left my mouth. I knew the answer. We were human calculators, and I'd watched him study my body the day before.

He lifted a brow, as if he was saying I didn't need an answer to that question. "There are two rules you must follow. The rear wheel and the exhaust system on this bike are covered. That said, you'll still keep your feet on the pegs until I let you know it's safe to remove them."

"Got it," I told him.

"And you'll hold on to me while you're seated on the bike," he added, stepping close to me again, the heat of his body escaping from his open jacket and seeping into mine. His arms were at his sides.

The lesson. He was testing me.

I placed my hands on his leather-covered biceps, consenting to his touch.

He pulled our bodies together, his hands gripping my waist.

"We'll be quite close, as we are now. You must hold on to me, Katie. Move your body with mine."

Again, I lost myself in his eyes, standing on that Manhattan street curb. I didn't want to be found. I didn't want him to release me from the command of his white-hot stare.

More heat moved through me. His or mine—I didn't know. I knew only that I ached from it and that he was the variable and the solution, the most beautiful mathematical equation.

"I will," I said.

He could see me, I thought. *All of me*.

Thomas abruptly dropped his gaze and backed away from me, breaking our connection, as if he'd read my thoughts and they had burned him.

six

THOMAS

I CHECKED THE GODDAMN HOUR AGAIN, THIS TIME USING the decorative clock above the dry bar cabinet in my living room.

Keeping time was becoming a compulsion, a new behavior for me that had Katie's name written all over it.

Katie. She hadn't replied to my text messages, to my dinner invite.

That morning at the coffeehouse, I'd allowed her to deny me her last name, her address. No questions, no prying into her family background, no searching for her personal details. I'd agreed to those terms.

In truth, the information would be quite easy for me to find. I'd spent years working for my father and my brothers, aiding their missions by hacking into government and private networks to acquire data and locate people.

But I had given her my word, and I would keep it.

Katie's request worked for me as well.

I wasn't prepared to discuss the shit I'd done in the past, the crimes I'd committed, the men I'd beaten, threatened, or the lives taken in the name of my family. I didn't want to tell her how darkness lived in my soul.

She was perceptive. She would see it.

Good. Let her see everything through her own eyes, I thought.

She needed to know my sins, so she could choose to live with them or run from me.

"Reed has no obvious affiliation to any political organization that would tie him to the prime minister," my brother said, his voice as clear as if he were standing in front of me rather than thousands of miles away.

Christ, I missed him. Will and I were close, and we operated on a level that resembled a well-oiled machine when it came to our father's field training. He was the one person I'd always been able to count on. He'd protected me from our father, taking the lion's share of the old man's cruelty onto himself.

And I'd thanked my brother by hurting him.

He forgave me for allowing myself to develop feelings for his wife, trusted me to work that shit out of my system. And I had purged those inappropriate feelings, recognizing that my admiration for her was quite different than the intense connection that had nearly wrecked me when I first saw Katie.

I was still forgiving myself.

I poured and finished two fingers of Macallan in one swallow, hoping the burn would punish me.

"His father was British," I said, trading the empty whisky glass for my mobile phone. "I'll investigate that angle and look into the connections his father might have had before his death. My gut says, Reed is in possession of some damaging information, and the prime minister wants it shut down."

"Sounds about right. What approach are you taking with Reed's wife?"

"I'm heading to her office now. I want to know what her role is in this game. My sources tell me she's quite a political force. I can't imagine she's uninvolved while her husband is engaged in matters linked to the prime minister, a man who's so deeply rooted in politics."

"One more thing, Thomas. The director general mentioned the Reeds have a child. As the investigation progresses, if the situation requires it, provide protection detail for the child. I don't give a fuck what the Reeds get themselves into or what happens to either of them in the end, but you keep that child safe."

We disconnected, and I turned my wrist to check the time.

Still no reply from Katie.

Another couple of fingers of scotch. My mood was spiraling. I tipped back and swallowed, opening my throat for the full pour.

The hour was early enough, and I planned to keep the meeting with Carolyn Reed brief. The rest of the evening could be turned round.

If Katie agreed to see me, the night would end well.

Before leaving my flat, I sent her another text message.

Tell me where to find you.

Nothing came back. No text-reply alert. No Katie.

I grabbed my jacket and my helmet and headed down to the parking garage. Sprinting across the garage pavement, I jumped onto my bike and sped outside onto the street, into the light.

SUNSHINE FLOODED THE ROOM, WAKING ME AFTER LESS than four hours of sleep. The timer on the electric window blinds had failed again.

Clinking glasses and silver, the smell of coffee.

My housekeeper was bustling about in the kitchen.

Christ. I raised my arm, shielding my face from the daylight.

The night before had been rough after not hearing from Katie, and it had taken quite a lot to keep myself from giving in and searching for her. But as I'd sat in the tattoo shop like the miserable fuck that I was, I'd found a better understanding of the unexpected position I'd taken with her.

I was as desperate for Katie's trust as I was for her touch. Gaining her confidence was necessary if she were to choose to be with a man like me. So, in a manner that was completely out of character for me, I'd give her a taste of what I would sacrifice to have her, to make her choose me.

God help her, she was already mine.

I rotated my arm to look at the tattoo. A bird in flight, its wings spread wide. The third sparrow on my body. The two others on my chest represented strength and family honor. This one was different. It was a female, and she carried a delicate wildflower.

My father had taken me to get inked on my eighteenth birthday, my first—our family shield on my right shoulder. I'd been quite thrilled at the time, proud to follow in my brothers' footsteps and receive a Hastings rite of passage.

Looking back, I'd had no choice. I'd been his soldier.

No more.

I hopped out of bed.

My ink. My money. My power.

After hitting the shower, settling arrangements with Carl, and making a quick stop to grab some gear, I rolled up to the curb in front of Jack's Coffeehouse on my motorbike. I cut the engine, removed my helmet, and pushed my fingers through my hair.

Though it was the weekend, instinct told me Katie was inside.

Her mind worked like mine. She was a mathematician.

But I'd sensed that she'd grown up quite isolated, which meant the patterns she lived with in her head were often her only companions. The isolation combined with the habits she kept through no fault of her own equated to a rather small footprint.

My pretty little bird lived inside a cage, and she'd led me to it.

Pain sliced through the center of my chest, sharp, sudden, and then gone.

I needed to know why her family had insulated her from the rest of the world. She was beautiful. Brilliant. She deserved adoration, for fuck's sake, not separation.

I swung my leg over the bike to dismount but stayed there on the street. My plan didn't include going inside for coffee again. I needed to touch her.

Impatient, on edge, I reached into my jacket for my mobile phone. No fucking around with text messages this time. Katie would hear my voice and obey me.

She would come to me.

As I tapped on the screen to wake it, an incoming call popped up.

A smirk hit my mouth, and I said her name aloud.

Five minutes later, Katie stepped onto the pavement, and my breath caught up in my chest for a second. My instinctive drive to defend flexed, triggered by the turning heads, the gaping second looks.

Christ, she had no idea that she affected other human beings. The sheltered lifestyle she lived did more harm than good.

A violent urge rumbled in my gut, encouraging me to shove through the pedestrian traffic and secure her tightly in my arms, to keep her safe. I pushed back on the impulse and waited her out, waited for her to find me.

"Ride with me, Katie," I said, reaching for her hand.

She nodded and locked her eyes on to mine, revealing the same exquisitely painful combination of yearning and obedience that had nearly put me on my knees the day I'd first met her.

I grinned, drawing her close to me.

It didn't matter that she'd never ridden before. I'd assumed as much. The important thing was her willingness. She'd chosen to get on a bike with me, agreed to my plan, proving that the trust I wanted her to surrender was coming along.

After allowing myself a minute to take in the unintended sensuality of her bare shoulders, her berry-stained lips, I forced my gaze back to her eyes.

She was breathtaking.

Leaning in closer, I wanted to reassure her. And I wanted to taste her lips.

We were close, so close that I could feel the warmth coming from her body, but with Katie, I needed her to show me with her touch that she was all in with me.

I'd sensed her innocence from the first moment. Mathematics was everything, the only thing her parents had allowed her to experience. I wanted her to know how easily a few simple words could be twisted in the absence of physical intention, that she should give active consent to a man as well as verbal.

I gripped her neck with force, lowering my mouth to hers, not to kiss her, but in warning. "Understand, sweetheart, I'm not the kind of man you want to tease."

She deserved a kinder man. But it was too late for that. I no longer planned to back away from this, from her.

How clever she was, catching on so quickly, this time running her fingers over my jaw, cupping my chin while whispering about her desire for me to kiss her rather than placing an order from a menu.

I kissed her fingers first and then her lips, a hint of sweet coconut lingering there from her latte.

Once I outfitted her in the leather jacket and helmet that I'd picked up for her and advised her on how she would ride with me, how I wanted her body to fall into sync with mine, we found ourselves lost in our connection for a minute.

Her eyes were stunning. As I held her stare, they revealed the loveliest soul.

I'm going to ruin this woman, goddamn it.

My chest tightened. I pulled away from her.

Katie reached for my hand and curled her little finger round mine. "I want this, Thomas. Let's go to the park."

That small touch. Her soft, approving smile.

She was the light I needed to move forward with my life.

An impulse consumed me, and I lurched forward, jerking her face up to mine, tugging her bottom lip between mine, sucking, tasting, owning, inhaling her exhaled gasp. I wanted her mouth, all of it. But I'd wait until we were off the street.

She pressed her palm on my chest and smiled from beneath her lashes.

I winked and then twisted round to the bike for her helmet. Before putting it on her, I said, "Let's get on with our day, beautiful."

I positioned us on the bike, and as we passed through Central Park, looped round Morningside, and then rode north along the motorway toward Fort Tryon, Katie clung to me with her body pressed tightly against my back, her arms wrapped round my waist.

The closer we got to Tryon, the more relaxed she became, one of her hands moving about to explore my abdomen without ever releasing her hold on me, as I'd instructed.

I grinned. I could turn back and take her to my place right then, and she wouldn't stop me.

Take it slow, motherfucker. You'll scare her.

Katie was different than all the other women. Her mind was brilliant but also guided by empathy. Her body and her soul were pure—this I knew instinctively. The goodness about her soothed me, gave me peace.

It had killed me to pull away from her lips. Those lips.

Concentrate on the road.

The Fort Tryon sign appeared as we rounded a tree-lined curve.

Katie shouted out in excitement.

I shook my head, smiling.

She turned her head and rested the side of her helmet against my shoulder.

Having Katie's thighs squeezing my arse, her arms hugging my waist, feeling the exhilaration move through her as she experienced the freedom of the open road with me—the intimacy of it all was making me mad for her.

I needed her, and I needed her to want me.

Entering Fort Tryon, I maneuvered to the car park and cut the engine next to my Escalade, and then we removed our helmets. I'd meant to help Katie dismount, but she popped off the bike on her own and into my arms the moment I was standing as well.

"That was amazing, Thomas. I loved it," she said, her bright smile so close to mine.

"That makes me happy, Katie."

Nothing could have stopped me from kissing her. I pushed my lips against hers and spun us round in the sunshine once, twice.

I set her on her feet, touched her cheek with the back of

my fingers. "We'll eat something first, and then you can show me round this place. Are you hungry?"

"I'm starving. You brought food?"

"Of course." I winked.

My housekeeper and Carl had prepared everything.

I opened the Escalade and found the blanket I'd requested along with a basket that was packed with food for the day. A small ice chest, holding bottled water and sodas, sat next to the basket. After tossing the helmets and jackets inside, I grabbed our supplies and led Katie toward the lawns.

"Are you sure I can't help carry anything?" she asked again.

"No, Katie. You're not carrying shit. Ask again, and I'll put you over my shoulder and carry you as well."

She laughed and looped her arm through mine. "All right. I like walking, so you win." Her eyes and fingertips moved over the new tat on my arm. "Does it hurt? Oh, there's something covering it."

"It's a transparent dressing, quite like a waterproof bandage. There's a stinging sensation at the time, some sensitivity for a few days."

She moved gracefully as she took one end of the blanket to help spread it out, bending over to set the corner. Her sweater neckline dropped, and I caught a glimpse of the top of her breasts, pushed up by a lacy pink bra. Her hair swept round her shoulders then like a silky curtain, covering her chest. But in that fraction of a moment, my cock had responded.

I lowered onto my knees and pulled her down to the blanket with me. "There are some vegan options in the basket. I wasn't sure. We haven't talked about that, Katie."

"You mean, because of the coconut milk? I'm not vegan. It's a dairy allergy. I love to explore different foods." Katie dug into the basket with enthusiasm.

Christ, that smile had the ammunition to ruin me in one day.

Watching her methodically sort items and plate them for us, I tucked a strand of hair behind her ear. "You counted them," I said.

"The grapes, yes. Sometimes, I can't help it." She popped one into her mouth and then pushed one into mine.

I nodded. I would be damned to let another second pass without kissing her again. The food could wait. I needed her mouth more. I tugged on the ends of her hair just hard enough to let her know what I wanted.

She dragged her teeth across her bottom lip.

Ah, fuck.

If we weren't in a location with others nearby, I would have punished her with a hard kiss for that move. As it was, I gripped the back of her head and pulled her face close to mine.

"Thomas," she said softly, her breath sweet and warm on my cheek.

"You need to understand how this goes with me. I'm

not like the boys at university. I can be a real fucking bastard. But even on my worst day, Katie, no one could ever satisfy you better or give you more than I will."

A small gasp came from her perfect mouth.

I nipped at her ear before going on. "I promised to wait, to allow you to come to me about your background. However, there's one thing I need, and I will not wait for that …"

seven

KATIE

As if my voice had abandoned me, I only nodded at him, at Thomas. He had asked me an intense question, demanding an immediate answer.

We were face-to-face on the lawn at Fort Tryon, overlooking the Hudson River. One hundred eighteen blocks away from Jack's Coffeehouse. Five-point-nine miles. Nine-point-five kilometers.

"Say it," he ordered. "I want to hear the words, Katie."

All or nothing was who this man was. I knew it just as well as I understood what I was getting myself into. And yet there I was, falling harder. I supposed his demands might have intimidated others, but for me, God, it pulled me deeper into his presence. It made me want more from him.

Would make me do anything to be with him.

My stomach abruptly fluttered and then knotted. The

butterfly effect was all Thomas. The knotting was the damn lie. When he learned my truth, I would lose him.

He lifted my chin with his forefinger.

I sucked in a calming breath, releasing it onto his lips. Nodding again, I said, “Yes, I’m all in with you. Thank you for being so patient with me.”

His hand slid to the nape of my neck. As he kissed my lips, he grasped handfuls of my hair, and I sensed we were fighting the same battle—restraining ourselves from going further.

Thomas and I spent the next hour eating and talking about his home in England. It wasn’t too surprising to learn that he’d come from an old aristocratic family, a line of earls. His grandfathers and father and now, his older brother Will.

When he spoke, there was sophistication layered into it. I’d thought it was an Oxford thing at first. The refinement lapsed now and then but always returned.

He was demanding and had an exceptionally large ego, but the manners of a gentleman would often pop out of nowhere. Helping me in and out of my jacket, waiting for me to sit or walk first, opening my water bottle—thoughtful little things.

These characteristics didn’t match his appearance or his manner of arrogance. His English aristocratic upbringing had shaped that contrast.

“I adore how committed you and your brothers are to family,” I told him.

Thomas took my hand. "It's who we are, Katie. My brothers and I protect our family with our own lives." I must have blinked hard because he kissed my knuckles. "I don't mean to scare you. But it's important for you to know that about me."

A wave of relief washed through me, warming me on the inside like the sunshine warming my shoulders. "I get it." And I did. I slipped my fingers through his, lacing them together. "Can I show you the Cloisters? We're already close. It's just behind where your car is parked."

He kissed the back of my hand. "The Cloisters it is."

After dropping off our picnic supplies, we hit the wooded pathway leading to the Met's second museum, this one of medieval European architecture and gardens. It should have felt out of place in the bustling metropolis of Manhattan, but it didn't. It was one of the things I loved about New York. It was, at the same time, a tiny island and so large that one could get lost in its hidden gems.

Thomas held my hand, sometimes my arm, and sometimes, his warm hand rested on my lower back as we toured the exhibits. The tapestries, the manuscripts, the Gothic chapel, the monks' resurrected chapter house from the monastery of Notre-Dame-de-Pontaut.

As we passed through the Judy Black Garden, everything overwhelmed my senses at once. The heat of his eyes burning into my skin, the fragrance of blooming wildflowers, the sound of water flowing through the garden's central fountain, the way he growled my name.

I'm high, I thought. I hadn't taken anything, but I was high as a kite.

Playfully, I slipped away from Thomas, running past the fountain and into the cloistered sanctuary again. He chased after me, and I spun around a stone column a few times, embracing it with my arms while laughing.

"*Reviens-moi, petit oiseau,*" he said with an impossible grin.

He'd mentioned inside the chapel that he spoke French fluently.

Thomas peeled my arms from the stone, and as he maneuvered my body with his to position my back against the column, he ran his fingertips over my bare shoulder. His eyes followed his touch.

I shivered. Goose bumps blanketed my skin. "What did you say?" I whispered.

His eyes met mine, and he flattened his hands on the column, one on either side of my head. "Come back to me, little bird."

Small breaths rushed in and out of my mouth.

"Are you going to kiss me?"

"No, Katie, I'm not. I wouldn't stop before taking more than I should." He looked over his shoulder at the people walking by and then touched my bottom lip, pulling it down with his thumb. "This isn't the time or place. When it's right for us, you should know that I will own every goddamn piece of your beautiful body."

A current of warmth spread through me, creating a fire between my thighs, and again, my breath quickened.

"Good girl," he said with a smirk. "Imagine it, how I'll make you feel."

Turning the small backpack that he carried along on his shoulder, he reached in and extended a bottle of water to me, opening it first. One hand went back to the column, recapturing me inside his space. "Let's hit the Heather Garden. I'd quite like to see the other side of this park with you."

I accepted the water and placed my empty hand flat against his hard chest. "You'll need to move first. You're blocking the way."

We smiled—his was a smirk—and then he stepped to the side.

On our way and then as we walked through the gardens, I used my smartphone to snap photos of the early heathers, bees on spring flowers, him.

"Some of the color intensity might have been captured if I had my DSLR with me," I said, stopping to display the photo of the pink-drenched tulip meadow for Thomas.

After inspecting the photo, he stared at me for what seemed like forever and then brushed over my cheek with the back of his fingers.

"Your mobile's camera function is quite advanced. You've been hiding yourself from me, Katie. Your mathematical genius exceeds mine, but I do understand how your mind works. Tell me about the numeric expressions you see looking out over the meadow."

Thomas was an exceptional mathematician, and it had only been a matter of time before he linked all the signs to my gift. I'd known he would all along.

I swallowed hard and forced myself to keep eye contact with him while slowly shaking my head. "I don't want to tell you. I want you to know my heart first. The part of me you're asking to see right now, it's like a mask that I'm forced to wear. I don't want to wear it anymore, Thomas. Not when I'm with you."

Touching my cheek again, he smiled and nodded. "All right. I see you." He placed a soft kiss on my lips.

Had he read my mind? I couldn't have asked for him to give me anything more. Tears welled behind my lids. I didn't let them fall. I returned his smile.

His tone shifted for a moment. "You will not hide yourself from me, Katie. Asking me to wait before learning about your family is not the same thing."

I didn't respond, not with words. My words would have been lies. I dropped my forehead onto his chest and dug my fingers into his T-shirt sleeves, and he put his arms around me.

"Listen," I said against his chest before lifting my eyes to meet his. "Do you hear the music?"

He looked around and then brought his gaze back to mine. "It's up on the hill."

A little stone cottage restaurant with an open-air terrace

was nestled beneath a canopy of trees—the only food venue inside the park.

"Must be someone's wedding reception," I said.

"Come," he said, taking my hand. "Let's have a look."

We hiked up the back side of the hill and spied on the couple's reception from behind a tree. After the bride and groom cut their cake, a disc jockey announced a set of slow songs. Thomas hovered above me, smiling, and right away, I understood the mischief playing inside his eyes.

I laughed while shaking my head at him. "No. We can't crash their wedding."

He pulled me into the open, toward the crowd. I dug in my heels, but he was more than determined.

Near the parquet floor, Thomas stopped to speak to a heavyset man in a gray suit, five feet eight—same as me—thirty-two or three. I couldn't hear their exchange.

Thomas spoke louder as he pulled ten one-hundred-dollar bills from his wallet and handed them to the groomsman. "See that the couple gets half and our best wishes."

Then, he took me into his arms, and I melted into his embrace.

"This is a very expensive dance, Thomas."

He drew me closer, touching his forehead to mine as the song carried us into a slow rhythm. "I would give up quite a lot more, Katie."

"As weird as this might sound, my brain rests when you're close."

His blue eyes locked on to mine, and my pulse began to race. I licked my lips.

"Katie, what are you doing to me?" He shifted his position, putting a slight amount of space between our lower bodies. "It's the same for me, you know. My demons retreat when I have you near me."

In the moment, all I wanted was to stay with him. To know more about him. To feel him touching me everywhere, for him to push his erection against me instead of moving it away. But I'd gone too far, lying to him about something as important as my identity. Our time would have to end soon. It had to end.

"Please take me back to Jack's now," I said.

MONDAY MORNING, MY MOTHER JOINED ME AT JACK'S before heading back to Albany.

"I won't stay long, Katherine. One cup of coffee, and then you can get to your plans with Lena. I need to discuss something urgent with you," she started.

"Mom, look, if this is about Columbia again—"

"It's not. Just listen to me, darling, okay? I'm genuinely concerned."

"What is it then?"

She set her cup on the table and gestured for my hand, and I gave it to her. "I've decided it's in your best interest at this time to have a personal bodyguard."

My heart started to bang inside my chest, beating in triple frequency.

I swallowed hard. “Are we in danger?”

Her eyes darted around the room, and her finger twitched as she took hold of the cup again. “Katherine, you know our situation is complicated. Your father has mentioned the threats we’re receiving again. As a family, we need to be cautious and do whatever we must to protect it.”

I closed my eyes for a moment. If this was what I thought it was, powerful people were involved. On the other hand, chances of that danger reaching me were slim. But my mother and I agreed on one thing: our family was fragile, and we had to protect it.

Nodding, I asked, “When does the bodyguard start?”

“I’m meeting with someone today to wrap that up. I’m sorry, Katherine,” she said with a measure of remorse. “Let’s change the subject for a bit. Have you found a gown for the party? I’m so enormously proud of you, you know. There aren’t many young women who would ask to share their own spotlight with a charitable foundation …”

As she went on, my thoughts digressed. I didn’t want that bodyguard. I didn’t want anything that got in the way of time with Thomas. We’d texted but not really talked since our fairy-tale day at Fort Tryon. I had ended it abruptly, overwhelmed by guilt caused by my deceitfulness.

I missed him. His eyes. His warm kiss.

"Katherine?"

I sighed with resignation. "Yes, I'll take care of the dress today."

"Please have Walter take you and Lena to the new boutique I was telling you about. The two of you will love it. The owner is pleasant and accommodating. I'll call her from the car."

She stood to leave and dismissed me with a hug, answering an incoming call on her cell. I could hear her clipped tones as she waved good-bye over her shoulder.

Lena passed my mother on her way in. "Tell me everything," she said, taking my mother's seat.

"It was amazing."

"You already said that on the phone. I want more details."

"I told you everything about the park, Lena."

I'd filled her in about how he showed up on his motorcycle, had planned a picnic for us at Fort Tryon, about exploring the Cloisters, crashing the wedding. What I hadn't told her was that this man was quickly becoming an obsession for me and that I was afraid of losing him. That I would absolutely lose him.

"But you're right; there's something else."

She nearly bounced out of her chair. "Damn it, Katherine. You know I'm going through a dry spell. I'm living vicariously through you right now. Spill it."

"It's not what you're thinking. Lena, I've done something, and when Thomas finds out, he will never see me again."

Lena pulled a face. "Wow. And ouch. What exactly did you do?"

"He doesn't know who I am. I mean, not at all. Not even my real name."

"Okay, all right. So, you intended for this to be a hook-up. I wasn't feeling that, but if that's what you want, it's okay. What you did is like using a dating app."

Pain lurched in my gut. I pressed my palms there, one hand on top of the other, and shook my head. "You don't understand. Thomas sees all of me. I'm more than a prodigy in his eyes. I want that. I want him."

"Shit. Katherine. I've never seen you like this. You don't have any choice. You have to come clean, girl."

eight
THOMAS

THE DIGITAL SCREEN ON MY OFFICE TELEPHONE LIT UP, displaying an incoming call. In twenty seconds, Janie would ring in to transfer a call from Carolyn Reed. The governor wanted a second meeting. She'd emailed Janie to give advance notice.

Governor Reed had been tight-lipped during our first meeting, performing as if she might gain something from me in return if she agreed to trade information. I made it clear that wasn't the game. Before leaving, I had assured her that my ability to circumvent her political power was beyond compare, that I would soon have intel on her entire family.

Another meeting was pointless unless Carolyn Reed was now afraid of someone.

Janie rang in, as expected.

"Put her through," I snapped.

Christ.

I missed Katie like a motherfucker. The proof was in my spiraling mood.

She'd cut short our day at Fort Tryon.

Because I'd pushed her too goddamn hard.

I'd given Katie a choice, telling her that I would drive her back to Jack's, as she'd asked, either in my car or on the motorbike. Without any hesitation, she chose the closeness of the bike.

She held me tightly with her arms and squeezed with her thighs while keeping her hands inside my leather jacket for the whole ride. She kept one hand just below the waistband of my jeans and the other on my abdomen.

Our bond was getting stronger.

It was difficult to kiss her good-bye, not only to leave her there alone, but also to leave her at all. She dug her nails into the back of my neck and pressed her body against mine. The need in her eyes nearly broke me.

Madness set in as I rode away from her, every cell in my body commanding me to turn back, to follow her, to see with my own eyes that she'd made it home safely.

I'd forced myself to endure the madness. Only ever for her.

We hadn't talked since. She'd asked me to give her a few days.

I checked the time and then tapped on the screen to connect the governor's call. "Mrs. Reed. I'm quite certain our business ended when we met at your office."

"Hello, Mr. Hastings. Please, I'd like for you to hear me out." Her tone was less challenging, amenable even.

My watch again. Katie would be hitting the coffeehouse soon.

"Five minutes, Governor."

"Thank you," she said with as much calm as she could muster. "I mean it with the best of intentions and certainly with no offense when I say, I've learned more about your family. Not just about the financial connections, but political as well. I also now understand what you and your brothers are known for as it relates to matters of security."

"My family's history is hardly a secret."

"I can't tell you what my husband's been up to because I don't know. He often acts without thinking or explaining. What I can tell you is that I'm receiving death threats at my office, linked to his behavior."

"You're the governor of New York, and you expect me to believe you have no idea that your own husband is engaged in some form of political maneuvering. I have somewhere to be, Mrs. Reed. You have three minutes."

"Please, Thomas—Mr. Hastings. My family is in jeopardy. I have the full force of the state police to protect me. But my daughter has nothing. That's the reason for my call. You're investigating my husband, yes. But my daughter comes first, and I won't settle for anything less for her. I want you to protect her."

Bloody hell.

I'd hoped it wouldn't get to the point where protecting

the Reeds' child was necessary. There had been no credible threats on my radar at the time.

"I'm not a personal bodyguard. Hire a proper service for your family's protection. I'll look into the threats."

"I appreciate that, but please, consider protecting my daughter. *Please.* I'll email the information and set up a meeting with your assistant for later this afternoon."

After agreeing to review the governor's files, I launched out of my chair like a fucking madman. I headed to the car, directing Carl to drive me back to my flat.

Firing up my motorbike, I reasoned that going to the coffeehouse to have a look at Katie, to see for myself that she was all right, was quite normal. I planned to keep my distance and watch her only long enough to be certain. Five minutes. Three hundred seconds. More if necessary.

I sped away from the garage, weaving round the traffic, conceding that my behavior was indeed not normal and accepting the fact that I didn't give a fuck. I needed to see her pretty smile. Those eyes. That goddamn mouth.

Katie exited the coffee shop with a dark-haired girl just after I worked my bike into a tight spot at the curb a small distance away from the coffeehouse. The two of them jumped into the back of a town car.

I couldn't see Katie's face. I needed to know if she was happy.

An overwhelming impulse vibrated in my blood, compelling me to follow the car, to see where she was headed. To know who was driving her round the city.

I'd promised not to dig into her background, and I wasn't.

This isn't that, I told myself.

If she was moving about within the limited space she lived inside, I wanted to understand how small the area might be.

The car traveled southwest, twenty-two blocks along Fifth Avenue, stopping in Midtown for Katie and her friend to enter a dress boutique. So, Katie was staying within the boundaries of her small footprint, just as I'd thought.

While she shopped inside the boutique, I called my brother John in England and instructed him to access my computer system and run the car's plates.

"Give me a few minutes to get home. I'll text you with the info," John said.

"Be quick about it, John. Everyone there is well? How's Mum?"

"Everyone is fine. Mum is happy. She's busy, helping Ellie get ready for the twins. Do you want me to come over there, Thom? You know our brother won't mind. He's doing well. I know you worry about him. You'll see when you come home. It's like he's finally found a little peace."

"I'm quite glad to hear it. He deserves it after everything he's endured for the family. No need for you to come to New York. I'll let you know if that changes."

I called Janie then with instructions to have the staff go ahead with the morning meetings and reschedule any that I needed to attend in person. A pressing business matter outside of the office had come up.

Right or wrong, making me a sick fuck or not, Katie was my business now.

Sooner than expected, she left the dress boutique, pausing in the middle of the pavement among the pedestrian traffic, looking in all directions, as if she'd sensed someone watching her.

My heartbeat accelerated. I pressed a palm against the center of my chest.

What I might have given in the moment for her to catch me lying in wait while she'd been trying on dresses, for her to meet my eyes with hers.

Katie and her friend got into the car, and I followed them to an open-air bistro on the Upper East Side. At one point, Katie turned and looked in my direction, and it was again like she could feel the weight of my stare.

We were connected.

Blood flow rushed to my cock.

Katie was mine, and I protected what was mine.

Enough. You've seen her smile, heard her laugh. She's safe.

I pushed my hair back, put on my helmet, and hightailed it to my flat, where Carl waited with the car to drive me back to my office in the Financial District.

As my client stood to leave my office, I restated the benefit of our partnership. "The expansion capital investment will net us both quite a lot of money. We chose a company for you with well-defined operating investments and solid growth."

With Leland Jensen gone, I closed the door and popped into my email. A brief message from Carolyn Reed waited —one line, cordial, confident.

I unlocked one of the encrypted files she'd attached. Copies of printed and emailed death threats, transcribed notes from voice mail threats. The next file profiled four men. At the top of the digital file, she'd made a note.

The following four persons were surveilled by my own investigator. He found no connections. Please review.

I nearly didn't because I was an arsehole that way. I didn't work for the governor, nor did I give a shit about her family. I had one job to do, and that was to protect mine. But something niggled at me—a slight crisis of conscience.

I began scanning the profiles, examining the photos and the personal and criminal data. The last suspect on the file jumped out at me at once.

Shit.

The entire situation was about to take quite a dreadful turn.

Carolyn Reed's private investigator had had no means to see beyond the cover of profile number four. I had experience working inside the back channels of the British government, so I knew that four was an assassin.

The prime minister wanted Chris Reed dead.

My instincts had been spot-on. Reed possessed harmful knowledge about the prime minister, and the prime minister was desperate to keep it buried.

The goddamn director general had given my brother his word. No hits had been or would be employed.

Before getting on with the last file, I hit the loo and grabbed a glass of Macallan from the conference room cabinet. Returning, I checked the time, considered whether I would meet with the governor, and then unlocked the encrypted dossier on her daughter.

I pushed back in my chair, my mouth open and suddenly dry, blinking at the screen, my chest tightening. Gasping, I leaned forward to catch my breath while flexing my hands to release the tension in the arm and shoulder muscles that had involuntarily tensed.

I was in shock over the images on the screen before me.

Katherine Reed. She was my Katie.

The word stuck in my throat, strangling me as I tried to say her name.

She was seventeen, according to the file, turning eighteen in two days.

Fucking hell. She lied to me about vital information.

John's text hit my phone, adding salt to the wound.

The car is registered to Christopher

Reed.

I poured the whisky down my throat, grateful for the burn, and then pushed back in my chair again, staring at her image. My skin heated, anger feeding on my soul, burning me from the inside out. It was an irrational thought, but a voice inside me shouted that she'd taken something away from me, something that was mine. And I was fucking angry about it.

I wondered if there was any truth to her words at all, anything she'd told me.

There was only one way to find out, so I read the file.

Identified early as a child mathematics prodigy, Katherine Reed was indeed a Columbia graduate with multiple fellowship offers. There wasn't much in the file—or on the web for that matter—about Katherine Reed, math prodigy, as one might imagine. Her parents had used their influence to put a lid on the press associated with their daughter's genius.

There were other indicators in the file framing Katherine as an aspiring community activist, though her parents had limited her opportunities to express that part of herself, restricting the number of events she could take part in, thus diminishing her achievements.

Katie's gilded cage.

Everything I'd seen in Katie's beautiful eyes—her virtue, the longing, her lovely soul—it was all there before me on the screen.

But even the governor of the great state of New York couldn't protect her daughter from university news blasts and random social media posts. And Carolyn Reed certainly hadn't protected her daughter from men like me.

It had been so easy to pick up her daughter in a coffeehouse.

I closed the file and forwarded the email to my brother.

I would have to let her go.

Closing my eyes for a minute, I said her name softly. "Katie."

No more anger. No darkness. Only loss.

An emotionless state washed over me.

I'd gone numb from the loss of my Katie.

Shit!

The assassin. He was out there, looking for Chris Reed, and no one was covering Katie. Christ, she had been out in one of Reed's cars earlier that day.

After bolting out of my office and sprinting to the lift, I texted Carl. I wasn't waiting for the governor to show up for our meeting. I was going to her. From the car, I rang Carolyn Reed's Manhattan office. She was in a meeting but still in the building. "Tell her I'm on the way with an urgent matter and she's to wait there for me," I said to her aide.

The governor was standing near her office door when I arrived. "Come in, come in, Mr. Hastings."

I closed us inside. "I gather your office is secure, Mrs. Reed."

"Yes, of course. You found something in the files?"

"Where is your daughter now?" My gut clenched.

"Katherine is at home, in our penthouse apartment. I just spoke with her. She understands that she is not to leave. Chris owns the building. It's secure. And before you ask, I don't know where he is right now."

I nodded. My concern wasn't for Reed's safety. "One of the profiles your investigator turned up is a cover for a British assassin."

"Oh God," she cried, reaching for the edge of her desk to steady herself.

She was an attractive woman. Aged well with glossy blonde hair, like her daughter's. I could imagine Katie growing old gracefully in the same manner, but without the hardness Carolyn carried round on her shoulders. It was as though Carolyn Reed hid behind an invisible coat of armor, which hardened everything about her, including her eyes. Nothing like Katie's eyes.

My Katie. Mine. Still.

"I will protect your daughter. My terms. Nothing is negotiable."

Regardless of the circumstances, I could never walk away and leave Katie unprotected.

Carolyn straightened her back. If she was surprised by my tone, she didn't show it. She only nodded and said, "I need you for Katherine's sake, so I'll agree to your terms. I'm listening."

"Keep her in the penthouse until I'm properly guarding

her. No shopping, no walking about, not even to the coffeehouse, and I do mean it."

"But how do you know—"

"It doesn't matter how I know. Are you still listening?"

"Yes, I'm sorry. Please, go on."

"This assassin will be relentless. I want to be quite clear. It might come down to me taking him out. And you should know that if he comes after your daughter, that's an absolute. I *will* kill him. Put a cleanup crew on standby. If you don't have one, get one. This is your mess, and you'll clean it up."

Fear overwhelmed her features, filled her eyes. "Consider it done," she said.

"I'll send for two men to assist with security detail. I want complete access to your building's security. All systems, cameras, alarms, and anyone you employ on-site."

She nodded. "It's yours. Whatever you need to take care of Katherine."

"Good. Send someone to my office tomorrow with records, keys, codes."

"However," she added, almost like a soft footnote, "I'd prefer complete discretion in the presence of my daughter. I'd rather not draw attention. Can you and the others blend in? Appear as part of our usual entourage?"

I stared at her for a minute. "I'll do my level best."

"Katherine's eighteenth birthday is in two days. We're celebrating at the executive mansion with a charitable ball on Friday. It's black tie. You'll attend and start then. Yes?"

I swallowed hard. I hated this woman right now. Seeing Katie that way, as Katherine Reed, would kill me. But I needed to rein myself in and concentrate on a plan of action to keep her safe.

"I'll be there. Remember what I said. She stays inside the penthouse until I assume responsibility for her then."

Without another word, I turned on my heel to get the hell out of there.

"Oh, and Mr. Hastings?" she said to stop me in my tracks.

I only gave her the side of my face.

"Thank you."

With a curt nod, I left her to live with her fear.

As I climbed into the back of the Escalade, Carl was waiting with his usual cheerful greeting. "Where to next?" he asked.

I was already tapping in Will's number before Carl started the engine.

"Park and 61st, thanks."

Nothing could stop me now, not even the promise I'd made her. Katie's safety came first, and I was going to get a good look at her home.

Will picked up, though it was getting late in England. "I read the files and contacted Director Martin. He's gathering some intel on this side."

"You tell that arsehole to understand the goddamn mission before sending someone into the field. The prime minister wants Reed dead. Period. This has nothing to do with espionage. It's personal."

"I let him know he'd better get his shit straight, brother."

Releasing a deep breath, I said, "Yes, of course. I know."

"Tell me what you need. How can I help?" Will asked.

"Send Andrew Evans over, if you can spare him from your security team. John as well. I'll use John to run detail inside the Reed house, and I want him with Katie whenever I need to leave her."

The chances of my younger brother having to make a hit were low. He'd only be allowed to fight to protect Katie and himself. I hoped it wouldn't come to that.

"I'll send them both at once, but let's back up for a fucking minute. What I'm hearing is, you're involved with the Reed girl."

As if he could see me, I pinched the bridge of my nose and nodded.

"Thomas," he snapped.

I had mentioned Katie the day before, and he intuitively understood the motive behind my needing it to be John who stayed with her in my absence. It was the same reason he'd left Ellie with me. When it came to life-threatening circumstances, we trusted only our blooded brothers to guard our women.

"Yeah, I guess it's fair to say so."

nine

KATIE

My life was a series of patterns. The patterns had steady rhythms, and all the moving parts fit inside a tidy little space. That idea had always been intrinsically comforting for me, necessary even. Until the day Thomas Christopher had walked into Jack's coffeehouse.

With him, I lost count of my heartbeats. The vital organ in my chest fluttered out of control, elevating from the usual constant rhythm with abandon. He'd taken me out of my comfort zone. And for once, I didn't care. As in math, when one manipulated quantity, structure, and space, change occurred.

I was changing.

The way we'd crashed the wedding and danced was burned into my memory, imprinted on my heart. I needed only to close my eyes to re-create how well our bodies fit together, his soft words close to my ear, the warm scent at the base of his neck, his lips touching my skin.

It had been six days and forty-nine minutes since he'd left me at the curb, and I missed him desperately. It was my own fault. Pained with guilt and shame for what I'd done, the lies I'd told, I'd pulled away from him, asking for time.

But now, I needed to see him. To come clean, as Lena had put it. It was the right thing to do. I wanted him to know everything. I would tell him how hard I'd fallen, that I wanted him. Then, if he never wanted to see me again, I would get what I deserved.

I didn't know how to make that meeting with Thomas happen with the bodyguard coming on board.

My mother had invited the guard to my party in Albany, and he was waiting for me with my parents in the East Room of the luxurious Victorian mansion.

Once I hit the staircase, my privacy will be completely gone.

Mom had been right to be concerned. I was sure someone was watching us, that there had been eyes on me when Lena and I shopped for the gown I was about to wear.

The boutique owner had delivered my dress to the mansion before our arrival, and on-site stylists had taken care of my hair, makeup, and nails. I'd had highlights added to my already-blonde hair. The result was subtle but added shimmery depth to my long tresses.

As I took in my reflection before the full-length mirror, my thoughts turned to Thomas again. I wished he could see me tonight. I looked sophisticated, even a little sexy, I thought. Like someone who might hold his attention for longer than a day in the park.

Lena interrupted my thoughts as she came into the room. She'd been summoned by my mother. "Almost ready? I brought a little something to take the edge off." She winked.

My eyes darted to her hands as she revealed the open bottle of champagne she had been hiding behind her back.

"Lena! The chief of police is here."

"As if. He's in your mom's back pocket, and you know it."

She offered me the bottle, but I shook my head. Maybe being the governor's daughter made me too cautious.

"Suit yourself." She took a swig.

"How is it?" I asked, eyeing the damn bottle.

"Nice. Girl, it's your party—"

I snatched the champagne and pulled deep from the bottle. "You're right. This is my party. And this is nice." I took another drink before setting it on the dressing table. "Help me into the dress?"

Lena laughed. "Damn, I like the feisty new Katherine." She swept across the room to pick up my lacy pale-blue gown. "Turn and step backward into it."

"Remind me to make you my maid of honor," I teased while she zipped me up.

She gasped. "So, you've talked to him?"

"No, I just meant someday."

"Forget about him. This is your night. We'll have more champagne, you'll party your brains out, and later, we'll curl up in our pajamas and watch one of those horrible '80s movies. You know, *Pretty Pink Candles* or *Dirty Flash Dancing*."

I chuckled. Lena always had a way of making me feel better. "Somehow, I doubt a charity-event-slash-birthday soiree is the best place to party my brains out. But I'll try."

I smiled at her reflection in the mirror.

"You never know. I caught a glance at your new bodyguard, and oh my God, Katherine. Girl, he's so hot. Now, let's go down there and rock it because you're also hotter than hell. Who knows? I might get you both drunk and pull a little ménage à trois."

I laughed, almost snorting up the mouthful of champagne I'd just consumed. Leave it to Lena to put me at ease and help me forget about life for a while.

She went down ahead of me to let my parents know I was ready, as instructed by my mother.

Five minutes later, I was at the top of the stairs, hearing my name as it was announced like I was about to be presented to the Queen. Orchestrated music played as I made my way down the grand staircase one step at a time. My back was ramrod straight, and I held my chin just as I'd been taught. All eyes were on me, guests toasting and smiling up at me.

I put on my best pageant smile, doing everything in my

power to wear the proper mask while taking care not to trip on my gown.

As if drawn by a magnet, I spun my head left, and my eyes swept over the man in the midnight-blue tuxedo standing beside my father.

Thomas.

Power and strength. Eight. Infinity. Flashes of sapphire danced through my mind. Eight was a feminine number, which contradicted his remarkable masculinity.

The sight of him made me falter in my stride.

I grabbed on to the railing for a moment to recover and then continued down.

My mind shot to a thousand possibilities as to why he was there. In my confused state, I imagined he'd reached out to my parents and wanted to surprise me, or maybe he was really good at crashing parties, just like the wedding in the park. But then the cold realization hit me. Lena's words. The hot bodyguard.

Mom and Dad stepped forward to embrace me as I reached the bottom, and then they turned us to pose for photos. There wasn't a lot of press there, but a charity event called for some publicity. They completely failed to introduce me to my new bodyguard, keeping him at a distance, like he was part of the scenery.

A glance at Thomas broke my heart even more than if he'd disappeared from my life forever. His expression was impassive and stern, and he refused to make eye contact with me. All part of the job, I supposed.

My insides twisted into a tight ball.

Had he already been on Mom's payroll the day we reached for the same coffee at Jack's? Was he the one watching me?

Lena tucked her arm through mine and tugged me away from my parents. "I told you he was hot. Let's see if he follows us."

We made our way through the crowd, politicians and donors greeting me, offering me birthday wishes. Some pursued small talk with me, asking about Columbia and what my plans were for the future. I gave them all dismissive, practiced comments—something I'd learned from growing up as a politician's daughter.

"Is he following us?" I whispered to Lena.

She turned her head, pretending to wave at someone, and quickly snapped back to me. "Yes. He's prowling behind us like a lion."

"Lena! What am I going to do?"

She chuckled. "I told you what I wanted to do."

"I'm serious." I knew the mansion like the back of my hand and took Lena to a quiet hallway, where we could slip into an office. But they were all locked for the evening. "Bathroom. Now."

A few doors away was a spacious restroom with a small lounging sofa. I pulled Lena in and locked the door.

"What's going on, Katherine?"

I put a hand on my forehead. "This is bad. No, it's

fucking awful. I was going to tell him everything, Lena, I swear."

"Hey, come on. Talk to me. You never speak that way unless you're truly rattled."

Bracing myself against the marble vanity, I checked my reflection in the mirror. No mask, only me. "It's Thomas," I said quietly. "*He's* Thomas."

Lena touched on my arm. "Wait, do you mean … are you saying he's the bodyguard?"

I took a deep breath. I didn't want to say the words aloud. "I don't understand it, but yes, Thomas is the man waiting in the hallway."

She gasped. "No way!"

I responded with a small nod after shushing her, fearing he might hear us.

Lena's features went from shock to indignation to wicked. "Ooh, this twist makes it even hotter. Think about it."

"Really? That's what you have to say? Remember, I lied to him."

"You were aware that he was on your mother's payroll then?" She didn't wait for me to respond. "He lied too. And he's in a position of authority. Now, he's going to tell you where you can go, who you can see."

I leveled a hard gaze at her. *Where are my numeric expressions?* I needed the math to regain control over my life. I closed my eyes to see the numbers. "You are absolutely no help."

"Okay, look. You said he hasn't touched you, that his kisses were sweet, on the lips. So, either he kept his promise and just wanted to go slowly or he lied, same as you, and you're his forbidden fruit. Whichever it is, he totally wants you, and it's unbelievably hot."

"I wish I knew what he wanted," I said.

"Only one way to find out." She pointed her chin at the doorknob, daring me to turn it.

The truth was, I'd grown obsessed with Thomas. I wasn't sure there were any scenarios that would make me want him less. I was an adult, and we'd both withheld information, so why would I give him up now?

"Okay, you're right. I'll talk to him. Cover for me if my parents start asking where I've gone."

"Always."

When I emerged from the restroom, Thomas was leaning on the opposite wall, and his blue eyes burned into mine with a fiery glower. His stare was equal parts fury and carnal want.

I reached for his arm. "Go somewhere with me to talk privately?"

He slipped away an inch, just enough to dodge my touch. A storm bubble dropped into my stomach.

"Lead the way," he said. Cold and indifferent, a trace of conflict in his tone.

We found an alcove one level up, where I knew we wouldn't be interrupted. As we walked along the corridor, I pushed down all emotion, playing every part the stoic woman.

"Tell me the truth," I said. "The day we met—"

"I didn't know who you were, if that's what you're asking."

"Then, what's going on here? Why are you employed as my personal bodyguard?"

He pushed his hand through his hair as he stared at me. "I'll explain myself, and then you'll tell me why you lied to me."

"That's fair," I said softly. "But you do already know the reason."

He nodded. "I'm not a bodyguard, and I'm certainly not employed by your mother. What I do is quite worse. My family has a history of running security detail, but not in the traditional sense that might come to mind.

"My father was an intelligence agent for the British government. He served his own political agendas as well, so he trained my brothers and me to be his private soldiers. After my father's death, we continued his work to pay for his sins, to protect our family.

"What I told you about my education, my home, my company is true. I didn't share that I'm conducting a back-door investigation for a high-ranking official in the British government—payment to save my brother from prosecution. At the time, it didn't matter. I had no idea you were connected to the case until your mother supplied me with your records a few days ago."

It pained him as he spoke the words, like something deep in his soul was tearing, and it hurt me to see it. None of what Thomas had said explained why he was acting as my bodyguard if he wasn't one.

"I don't understand why you're here."

"Your father is the subject of my investigation, Katie. Whatever comes of it, keeping you alive is now my priority," he said.

ten

THOMAS

Katie gasped. "Someone is coming after my family?"

Christ, she was beautiful, even as her shoulders drew tight.

I'd already moved beyond her deception. I had forgiven her, I realized.

She's eighteen.

Age was a numbers game, as was everything else in life. But there it was, an obstacle standing between us, forcing me to consider what I would give up to save her from my ruin.

I'd kissed her lips. I hadn't touched her. The legal age of consent in New York was seventeen, so if we had gone further, it would have been lawful.

If we'd both been ten years older, if she'd had time to live freely and discover what she truly wanted, the gap would have meant nothing to me.

A gray storm roused in her eyes. She dropped her voice to a whisper. "Please tell me."

"I can't say why at this point, but a hit was put out on your father."

She nodded, as if she understood the reason for it. "And my mom?"

"Is concerned about you."

"How much do you know? I mean, do you know who it is?"

"It has come to a matter of life and death, but no one will hurt you, Katie, not while you're in my charge. That's all you need to know."

Whispering again, she said, "Because you believe I'm a child."

I lowered my gaze to her body, to the creamy-white skin between her breasts. "You're anything but a child."

Her gown was perfect, tucking in tightly at her waist before falling to the floor in a soft cascade of pale blue, leaving every man in her presence wondering what he might find beneath it, while exposing her neck, her shoulders, her chest.

No one else would get close enough to touch her.

Neither will you, arsehole.

"Then, kiss me," she begged. "I need you to kiss me."

Pacing round in the small space, I shook my head. "I can't. Not anymore." But I was mad with the desire to finally taste more than her lips. The erection I'd tried to tame strained against my trousers. I needed to touch her, mark her skin with my fingers, my mouth, push the hardness of my cock against her body.

"Nothing between us must change."

"Everything has changed," I snapped, stopping in my tracks to pin her with my eyes. "Being with me would ruin everything that's exceptional about you, Katie."

"That's not true," she said, stepping close. Her hands touched mine, and then she dragged her fingertips up the sleeves of my jacket until grasping on to my biceps. "You're still calling me Katie."

She was my Katie.

"You'll never be Katherine to me. I'll give you that. As for the rest of it, you don't know what you're asking of me, what you'll see."

She drew closer still, allowing her breasts to brush against me, the fire between us growing hotter, stronger. "I want to see everything, Thomas, to know all of you. I'm asking you to show me."

My breath accelerated.

She was surrendering the trust I'd desired.

It was more than I could bear. Her loveliness and innocence, calling out for me to pull it into myself—it was mine; she was mine. There was no help for it.

With my body, I moved her backward, caging her in, her back to the wall. I gripped her waist and pushed my rock-hard length against her body.

Katie took in a small, sharp breath.

I pushed hair away from her neck, bending to kiss her

below the ear. "This is what you do to me, Katie. You are so beautiful."

As she stared into my eyes, she popped open the buttons on my jacket and slipped her hands inside, resting them on my abdomen.

Brave little bird.

"My mother doesn't approve … of the dress," she said.

"You don't need her approval. You have mine."

Christ, the dress. Her skin. The sheer top resembled a deeply V-shaped stringer, molded to her body, her breasts obscured behind the see-through fabric by pale blue coverings. So much delicate skin available to me, to my mouth.

She nodded, and I placed another kiss on her neck, lingering, tasting.

She slid her hands round my waist and pulled on me, increasing the pressure against my cock. An involuntary primal grunt rumbled in my throat.

An internal battle waged inside me. My compulsive, selfish nature to take what I wanted won the fight. It always fucking won. I claimed her, parting her lips with my tongue, allowing myself to finally taste her sweet mouth. There was no turning back.

Katie moaned as I explored every soft crevice of her mouth.

My kiss was brutal, not gentle, as it should have been.

For her sake, I reined myself in, trailing soft, apologetic kisses down her neck and over her shoulders. She panted and held on to me. I was quite lost in her, lost in the euphoria of holding her in my arms and controlling the movements of her body with mine.

She melted into me, her body taking on the shape of mine. That we fit together so well pushed me over the edge. I took her mouth again, fierce and hot as she writhed against me, my erection hard as steel against her stomach.

I wanted to bury myself inside her, make her come again and again.

Guilt abruptly overwhelmed me, and I stopped.

"Don't stop," she said, unable to hide her ragged breaths. "Please."

Goddamn it.

It killed me to see her so deliciously responsive and breathless. But even if our circumstances were different, she deserved better than a quick fuck before her birthday cake.

I dropped my arms. "I'm sorry. I shouldn't have—"

Grabbing my jacket as I backed away from her, she used it to pull close to me again. "Don't you dare say it. We're still the same two people who shared that amazing day at Fort Tryon. We're still free, still us."

I shook my head and flexed my fingers at my sides, drawing them into fists. "We're not. Don't ask me for this, Katie. There's nothing but hurt and pain down that road. I won't drag you along with me." I drew my thumb over her bottom lip and then to the corner of her mouth to wipe at a smear of lipstick.

Any excuse to touch her again.

Her hands went to her hips, and her shoulders straightened, reminding me of how spirited she'd been the first time we met at the coffeehouse. "I'm perfectly capable of choosing which road I'll travel and with whom. I'm not giving up on us."

"Quite right. You deserve to choose the life you want. Being in a relationship with me would be like moving from one prison to another. I'll protect you, and when my job is done, make no mistake, Katie, I will leave."

Like the damn prick that I was, I turned on my heel and walked away from her, away from the hurt in her eyes.

She was young, but quite worse was what a possessive motherfucker I was. She could never be free with me. I would own her. Ruin her.

"You have two hours to enjoy your party, and then we head for Manhattan," I added over my shoulder as I waited outside the alcove while she righted her dress. I turned to catch a side-glance. It was compulsive. I had to see.

But I would keep my hands to myself, moving forward.

She pulled her fingers through her long blonde hair, untangling the locks where my hands had been, and a sudden tightness struck my chest.

Mine. Can't let her go.

eleven

KATIE

THOMAS CLOAKED ME INSIDE HIS TUXEDO JACKET, securing it around my shoulders, and rested his hand on my lower back as he guided me to the executive mansion's rear private exit. He'd been true to his word. Precisely two hours after informing me that we were leaving my party early, we walked out the door to find his driver waiting for us.

He tucked my dress and me into the back of his car and drew the seat belt across my body, as if I couldn't do it myself. "Always wear it, Katie. Even when you're seated in the back."

While slipping off my stilettos, I noticed he wasn't doing the same for himself. "What about you?"

"I must be prepared to move without a moment's notice." His eyes locked outside the window beside me, his manner of speaking cold, all business.

The dangerous vibe he'd emanated at Jack's was not only back, but also evolving into a more severe, darker mood. There was more to this man than I understood.

I shivered. A fluttering sensation dropped from my pounding heart into my gut. It didn't stop there. It rushed lower in my abdomen, to the core between my legs. I closed my eyes and pressed my thighs together, squeezing to keep the feeling there inside me, wanting the blissful little ache to stay forever.

God, I was turned on.

Thoughts about how he'd kissed me in the alcove raced through my mind. His hand grasping my hair, pulling back my head. The earthy taste of scotch on his tongue.

"Katie," Thomas snapped.

I jerked open my eyes. "I'm sorry, what were you saying?"

He stared at me for twenty-two-point-five seconds before saying a word, his irises stricken with something that resembled tiny lightning bolts. Captivating light-blue eyes morphed into the same pale color of my dress. "Don't fucking do that," he finally said.

"Do what?"

"You know what I'm talking about."

I sighed and dragged my gaze away from where he adjusted his trousers. "Do you keep anything in here to drink?"

Thomas leaned forward and pushed his fingertips against a panel. It swung open, revealing a hidden bar. He pulled out a bottle of water, opened the cap, and offered it to me.

"Something other than water, please." Ignoring the bottle in his hand, I leaned in as far as the seat belt allowed to see inside the cabinet. Scotch. Dom Pérignon. Small crystal glasses. "A glass of Dom would be nice."

"No." He shoved the bottle of water closer, near my chest.

"I'm not interested in your Evian right now."

"No more alcohol," he growled.

"What do you mean?"

"I'm being quite clear. I tasted you earlier, Katie, and I'm familiar with champagne on a woman's tongue. You've had enough."

My stomach clenched, and a cold, unthinking response escaped me. "So, now, I'm a child again."

I shouldn't have said it. He'd implied that I was a woman. He'd also pointed out that he'd tasted many other women. That had been the trigger, and I didn't know how to sit with the newest emotion rolling through me —jealousy.

Quickly, I added, "Fine," and accepted the water bottle.

Our fingers touched for a moment before he drew his hand away.

With his eyes diverted back to the cars moving outside my window, he said, "I've made my position on that matter clear as well."

"Then, why? I mean, really. You see it in the UK all the

time. Drinking is legal even before eighteen over there, right?"

Eyes back to me, his stare burned white and hot. He shook his head and then checked his watch, trading one intense reaction for another. "Stop making everything about your goddamn age, Katie. I'm not opposed to you sipping a glass of champagne when the time is appropriate."

"Oh," I said stupidly.

"You're correct; it's legal in England, even at sixteen in some cases. I've seen quite a lot of young women get pissed just because they can. It's not attractive." His tone softened. "You're too lovely for that."

I blinked and then dropped my eyes, my voice. "I'm sorry."

"*I'm sorry* isn't a phrase I want to hear you say again, not to me." The softness of his demeanor faded, and the unyielding bodyguard returned. "Put on your shoes. We're transferring to the governor's helo in three minutes."

Hee-low. A pronunciation that screamed of the military-style training he'd received from his father.

We got out of his car and hopped into the helicopter, just as he'd said. Sixty-five minutes and thirty-two seconds later, we landed on a rooftop in Manhattan.

Marta was waiting in the foyer when we stepped out of the penthouse elevator. Meeting her eyes with a slight nod, Thomas slid his hand down my back and let it fall away. Marta rushed to me. She removed his jacket from my shoulders and handed it to him without uttering a single word, replacing it with her warm arm as she guided me down the hallway.

"Mom told you about everything. And about Thomas?"

"I talked with your mother and your father this morning. It's why I didn't attend your party, Katherine. I'm sorry I missed it. I wanted to see you and Lena, but it was more important for me to be here when you arrived home with *Mr. Hastings*."

Her emphasis on *Mr. Hastings* was meant to correct me.

Marta was perceptive. She'd raised a beautiful, free-spirited daughter. I was inexperienced with relationships and with hiding my interest, but the same wasn't true for Lena, and Marta was well aware of that.

I looked back over my shoulder at Thomas. He locked his eyes on to mine and held our connection until I disappeared into my bedroom.

I WOKE TO ANOTHER SUNLIT NEW YORK MORNING, sunshine bleeding through the sheers that hung in front of the glass terrace doors. Warm rays sliced through the center where the panels were supposed to meet and landed on my bed.

Thomas had drawn the curtains before closing the door and leaving me alone in my room for the night. I'd opened them at once. The space became dark and closed in when the draperies were shut, and it made me anxious, as if I were trapped.

Imprisonment. I'd never been able to pinpoint the source of my discomfort or at least I hadn't put a name to it. Thomas had called it a prison.

Right on cue, my phone buzzed, dancing around on the nightstand as it vibrated to announce my mother's call.

She had agreed with Thomas that it would be better for her and Dad to stay on in Albany. Security had been tightened up at the mansion, but Thomas believed I was safer at home, detached from the principal danger.

Death threats were getting more ominous and frequent. A bomb squad was on twenty-four-hour alert, and all calls were traced by the state police. Guards flanked the entrances and went with Mom everywhere.

If my father stayed close to her, he would be protected as well.

I grabbed my phone and swiped to answer. It was earlier than usual for her to call. "Mom, is everything all right?"

"I'm sorry, Katherine. I know it's early. All is well here. I spoke with Thomas this morning. And Marta. But I wanted to hear your voice for myself before my meetings. Are you still in bed, darling?"

"Yes, but you didn't wake me."

"Please stay in and listen to Thom—Mr. Hastings. I trust him. No one is more qualified to be your guardian at this time."

I corrected her, "Guard, not guardian. I'm eighteen. I no longer have a guardian."

"Really, Katherine. Don't be difficult. Please just do as you're told. I can hardly go to the restroom alone. I expect the same kind of protection for you. We can't be certain, but it's possible you might be in danger as well. We just can't be sure."

Little did she know of the real jeopardy I faced. The danger for me was about losing my heart completely to Thomas, embracing the darkness he was gradually revealing, and becoming submissive to our mutual desire.

Time to change the subject. "Would you tell Dad to call me? How is he?"

She cleared her throat. "He stepped out first thing."

"What do you mean, he stepped out? He's supposed to stay close and share your protection detail."

"When I see Chris, I'll tell him to call you. I need to run. Maya's waiting for me. Listen to Mr. Hastings as you should, Katherine. I'll miss you this week." My mother disconnected.

A meeting with Maya Williams, the lieutenant governor, was more important than discussing my father's safety. Sometimes, she could be so damn cold.

Eager to talk to Thomas, I hit the shower. He would know what was going on with my father. When I came out of the bathroom, a tall paper cup from Jack's Coffeehouse waited for me in the center of my photography worktable.

I removed the cup's plastic lid and inhaled deeply

through my nose. Coconut milk. Espresso. The sweet caramel-like scent of brown sugar.

He remembered.

Four misplaced photos jumped out at me as I sipped the latte. Wildflowers at Fort Tryon. One of the profile shots I'd taken of him. Two selfies—one with him kissing my temple. I held my breath for several seconds, remembering that kiss, remembering how it had caused a fluttering in my stomach, how it had been followed by another one on my lips.

I'd placed all photos in perfect order on my worktable, and he would have recognized that. He wanted me to know that he'd looked at them.

As if my thoughts had the power to summon him back, he knocked on the door. "Katie, come to the dining room."

A thrill rushed through me at the sound of his voice, and I smiled.

Damn it, no.

Clear boundaries had been set.

After everyone had settled in the night before, Thomas had given me a verbal list of rules. Draperies closed. Doors locked. No visitors. No attending the commencement ceremony. Ask his permission to make important appointments, and if he agreed, follow his instructions. What was more, he'd said that he wasn't going to touch me again.

I looked at my hands and gripped the paper cup more tightly. "I'll be there in a minute."

When I entered the room, Thomas looked up from the

laptop in front of him, and a shadow passed in front of the blue in his eyes as he stared at me. It was the first time I'd seen it in him—darkness overwhelming his emotions. He'd successfully hidden that part of himself from me.

The energy between us was intense. It twirled in the air like a little hurricane, pulling me in, revealing how he wanted me, cared for me, craved me.

A quiver ran along my spine, and I wrapped my arms around myself.

"Are you all right?" he asked, a hint of tenderness in his voice.

My knees weakened. I dug my nails into my arms.

Thomas commanded things, told people what he wanted, what they wanted. I couldn't recall hearing him end one sentence with the intonation of a question. Something prevented him from doing it—his ego or his upbringing or something else that I didn't know.

He'd just done it for me.

Before I could answer, he stood and said, "I've scared you."

Closer, he came around the table, so close to me.

I lowered my eyes, stared at the floor.

Using his bent forefinger to lift my chin, he forced my eyes back to his. "I did warn you."

"That's not it." I wasn't afraid of him. "You couldn't possibly understand."

"Try me, Katie. Trust me with it."

Shaking my head and squaring my shoulders, I lied to

him again. "I don't want to trust you. You don't want to continue our relationship, so there's no reason for me to trust you with anything." Growing angrier, I pushed his hand away. "And please, do me a favor. Stop looking at me like you want to fuck my brains out. Seeing that does not help, Thomas."

Hurt filled his eyes for a fleeting moment, and then he nodded. "You're quite right. I can't look at you any other way, so I'll maintain more distance."

I narrowed my eyes. "Denying your feelings doesn't make you a hero. It makes you a huge asshole for hurting mine." I spun and walked away.

Restless, insecure, wounded, I used the whiteboard wall in my room to regain control. After hastily erasing everything, I began scrawling a list of natural even integers and showing each as the sum of two prime numbers.

Goldbach's conjecture. The theory plagued mathematicians with one simple question: was it true that the list carried on infinitely? It remained unproven, though some had said that if the conjecture was unprovable, then it must be true.

I often used the exercise to comfort myself.

But my mind continued to reel with thoughts about how to change Thomas's position. So, I scribbled faster. More integers, more primes. It didn't help. I threw the marker at the wall.

Exercise. I needed to walk. The penthouse was five thousand eight hundred square feet. Eight hundred thirty-five thousand two hundred square inches. Two thousand three hundred twenty steps from one end to the other.

Walking outside had always been part of my routine, a reliable constant. I could stretch and think and breathe in the fresh air. Sometimes, while strolling around my own small piece of Manhattan, I pretended to be in another city, in another part of the world.

I couldn't hold back the need to move, to catch a sense of freedom. My wanderlust needed some relief.

Thomas knocked. "Katie, I want to talk to you."

I finished tying the laces on my sneakers, stared at the door for a minute, and then sighed. Why couldn't I stay mad at him? "Come in."

He looked around the room. His eyes hit the open draperies, the whiteboard, my shoes. Finally, his gaze burned into mine, and he said, "You're not going anywhere, little bird."

twelve

THOMAS

I HAD WORKED QUICKLY TO INCREASE SECURITY AT THE penthouse, ordering the installation of more cameras to cover the entire building and the parking garage as well as upgrades to the existing monitoring equipment.

John and Andrew Evans were due to arrive in several days. Evans had been a soldier in the Royal Army before joining Will's security team. His loyalty to my family was irreproachable. With their aid, I could get out in the field to track the prime minister's assassin and deal with Reed's sudden disappearance as well.

Pushing my hand through my hair, I cursed.

Because now, every move I made affected Katie.

If her father had committed espionage against the British government, she would hate me for turning him over to MI5. But I had no choice. I had to follow through for my brother's sake, no matter the personal cost to me.

Completing this mission was the least of what I owed him.

Katie was unaware of Reed's missing status. She'd stormed out of the dining room, and I'd allowed her to go without telling her, deciding to first give her space to deal with her anger.

Christ, how I ached to touch her. Being so close, confined in the same living quarters, practicing restraint. It was an agony worse than any military tactic.

What was more, emotional attachment transcended my physical desire.

Kissing her, holding her in my arms at the executive mansion, feeling her respond to me as she had. There had been more than sexual need in those moments.

Clarity came to me while I watched the sun rise from my position on the brick-paved terrace. Leaning against the iron railing with my coffee in hand, lights of the city fading into the rose-colored dawn, I conceded. I'd been lying to myself.

Letting Katie go had never been in the cards.

I cared for her deeply enough that I would find the strength to wait, giving her time to explore the freedom she deserved before taking it away. There was no turning back. There was only time.

Katie needed to know. I had to make her understand.

Tautness struck my chest. Self-reproach. I would still ruin her.

I glanced at the clock on the wall. Forty-five minutes

had passed. My heartbeat raced. I was desperate to see her again, to find another reason to touch her.

She'd been quite upset, I thought. *And she's alone.*

Determined to put her at ease, I went to her. I found her sitting on the edge of her bed, tying the laces on her trainers, as if she were going out. She met my stare and nailed me with the longing in her eyes that had become my weakness.

"You're not going anywhere, little bird."

Katie tested me with her defiant wit and beautiful smile. "Whatever would give you that idea?"

"You never wear trainers indoors. You wear slippers or nothing at all."

"You're very observant, Mr. Holmes, but I'm afraid now"—she slapped her shoes on the hardwood floor and stood up—"the game is afoot."

"This is not a goddamn game. You don't know what dangers await you."

"This is New York. It's dangerous to cross the street."

There was her headstrong defiance again. I pinned her with my eyes to convey the potential dire repercussions of leaving even if for a few minutes.

She dismissed my warning with a flippant shake of her head. "I promise not to cross the street, okay?" Extending her hand, she added, "Just a trip around the block. Come along with me."

"We're not going for a stroll, holding hands, if that's what you're suggesting."

"You don't have to be an asshole. It doesn't help at all, you know. I can see that you want to touch me. You can. I want you to."

I stalked farther into her room, moving closer with each word. "I have to wonder how many times you've said those words, Katie. You know nothing about men. How we think. What we want. What bastards we can be when a woman teases us."

Her fitted white T-shirt clung to her, revealing the curves of her breasts, and a diamond pendant in the shape of a delicate star lay against her chest at the bottom of the V. I had to touch her skin. I dragged my fingertips down her arm.

"I'll be sure to avoid them then. On my walk," she half-whispered.

Irritation surged through me. I latched on to her wrist and growled, "I said, you aren't going anywhere."

I wanted to scare the shit out of her, so she'd stay put. Force her compliance.

A gasp escaped her mouth, her pretty lips forming a circle. She recovered quickly, disobedience flashing in her eyes. "Try and stop me," she challenged.

I smirked. Yanking her wrist up, bending her elbow, I crashed her body into mine, my arousal hard as stone against her belly. "It would take nothing for me to overpower you, to do whatever I wanted with your body."

"What?" she breathed.

"Fight me," I demanded, tugging harder on her wrist.

"Defend yourself. You want to travel? Then, you must understand how dangerous it is out there. What men can do to you. Men like me."

Little did she know, there was truth in those words. That *men like me* meant me as well, the bastard abusing his authority. Charged to protect her while lusting after her. Needing her. Falling asleep at night, thinking of her with only the poor company of my own hand.

Her lips parted again, and I knew I was losing the battle. She was the one owning me. She touched me, reaching down to wrap her little fingers round my cock and squeeze.

Fuuuck.

I was quite prepared to die for the woman I'd waited for my whole life, but I never imagined I'd take my last breath in this way. She was killing me with those fingers, her clumsy palm, rubbing me into madness. And her perfect face, those tempting lips, stormy eyes dancing over my features, as though she could read my thoughts.

No more. I threw her on the bed, facedown on the mattress beneath my weight, splaying her arms over her head and cuffing her wrists with one hand.

"Fight me. You can leave if you can show me that you can defend yourself."

I rocked into her arse, taking pleasure from her softness. Establishing dominance. Proving my point.

She raised her hips to meet my erection.

"Fight me," I grunted, plowing against her, showing her

how much stronger I was. How much stronger any man would be. How defenseless she was in that position.

It felt too good. I wanted our clothing gone. My hard cock against the smooth skin of her arse, my fingers inside her, drawing wetness out of her. I wanted to thrust into her. How fucking amazing it would be to fall into ecstasy with her, climaxing together again and again and again.

"Say no. Tell me to stop, Katie," I begged.

I wouldn't be able to stop on my own. Not while she was consenting. I needed her to tell me no. But she wouldn't say it. She wanted me as much as I wanted her.

Desperate to taste her skin, I licked her neck.

"Yes," she cried. "I don't want you to stop."

She continued resisting my warnings. I flipped her onto her back and pinned her arms above her head again, driving against her with more force, getting off while punishing her for her insubordination. Looking into her eyes while pressing myself against her nearly pushed me to the brink of insanity.

I wanted to lock the door. Tie her to the bed. Open her legs with my knees and drive myself between her thighs. I wanted to take her in every conceivable way. To devour her and ruin her.

My control was slipping. I had to bring us both back to the lesson.

"I mean to teach you," I said, hoping the defiance I'd seen earlier would emerge. I took the skin on her neck into my mouth, wanting to suck, to kiss her there. I bit her, just enough to leave a mark. I wanted to leave my mark on her. "Fight me, goddamn it."

Still, she didn't oppose me, didn't answer violence for violence. It occurred to me then that the only censure I could impose on her would be to make her crave me, to yearn and grieve for my touch as much as I yearned for her.

Holding her wrists a fraction more tightly, I forced my body still. I kissed the mark on her neck with tenderness, dragged my lips to her ear, and rumbled, "When you allow a man to have you, Katie, you're giving him the greatest gift he'll ever receive."

I peeled myself from her warmth with agonizing torment, leaving her panting and flushed. Walking away hurt me more than it hurt her. But it was necessary.

"Take off your trainers, Katie. You're not going out, not today."

thirteen

KATIE

THOMAS HADN'T ALLOWED ME TO LEAVE FOR THREE DAYS. Seventy-two hours, locked up inside the penthouse, felt like weeks. I missed Lena's company. I'd pleaded with Thomas to send his driver for her, but he wouldn't let her come, wanting to keep her out of the line of fire. When he'd put it that way, Marta and I had agreed.

Aside from that and discussing my father's situation, we'd hardly said a word to each other. Dad was missing, and not knowing my father's whereabouts weighed heavily on us both. I could see his thoughts spinning behind distant eyes, and he noticed the horror in mine.

"I'm so sorry, Katie," he said, drawing me against his broad, hard chest to comfort me. "I'll search for him as soon as John arrives. I will find him."

His younger brother, who was also eighteen, was flying

in from England to help guard me and free up Thomas for the investigation.

To reassure me further, Thomas explained there was still hope even if his findings forced him to turn my father over to the British government.

"Reed"—as he'd been referring to my father—"is an American citizen, and because your parents have quite a lot of political influence, the US government could seek extradition before he's prosecuted in the UK. If he has committed espionage, it would be more helpful for him to be charged and tried here."

Thomas was in a difficult position. I couldn't fault him for doing what was necessary to protect his own family.

"We'll ring your mother and speak with her together," he added.

Not even a full minute into the call, Mom swept into one of her stoic performances. We were discussing my father's disappearance, for heaven's sake.

Her lack of emotion made me wonder, *Is she keeping important details to herself? Does she know where he is and what he's doing?*

After getting nowhere with her, we disconnected the call, and Thomas turned to view the security monitors.

"So, will you allow me to go to the studio today?" Despite the awful situation, one obligation still existed that I needed to fulfill, and it required me leaving the apartment.

I stood there in the dining room with Thomas, staring at

the hard sheet of muscle on his back, waiting for a response to my request.

A minute passed, and then he spun, crossed the room, and hovered close. A move that made me weak. He consistently approached me like a predator, and I wanted him more each time he did it. His navy-blue T-shirt hugged his chest muscles as well.

"Of course. You must do it," he said, surprising me.

I'd been offered Columbia's fellowship for excellence in mathematics, a completely funded package, but it came with the stipulation that I took part in a charitable program to benefit dyslexic children.

The organization planned a video campaign, and my role was to demonstrate the application of basic math skills, using a system that dyslexic kids could grasp. I'd collaborated with my professor to create the plan before graduation.

The campaign's overall format was groundbreaking, joining mathematics with music and art. With the way my brain associated numbers with color, assigning shades and notes to mathematic expressions came easily for me.

Lessons created by me would integrate into the full story. The project editor planned to splice my prerecorded presentation into short clips and drop them throughout the video series.

I'd received the offer from Oxford before the project reveal, but it hadn't mattered. Zero. That was how many regrets I had for my contribution to Columbia's dyslexia campaign. I enjoyed community activism, and I was pleased to take part in any project that advocated change for the educational systems that unfairly affected disadvantaged children.

"I'll make it happen," Thomas added.

I smiled. "Really? You did hear the part about me going to the studio, right?"

He nodded. "I'll figure out the logistics." A smile curved one side of his mouth, and he dragged the back of his fingers over my cheek. "I won't hold you back, Katie. Your parents have kept you from your dreams, but no more, not on my watch. Seeing you smile like this, how it lights up your eyes, it makes it quite worth the pain it'll cause me to let you go."

The pain it will cause him to let me go. But he sees me. He still sees me.

"Thank you." I grabbed hold of his hand as he dropped it. "Now would be a good time to kiss me—if you fancy kissing me, as you would say."

He lowered his forehead to mine and said hoarsely, "I do. But I won't."

"And I won't give up," I whispered.

"I know," he breathed.

Our lips were close, so close. His warm, masculine scent overwhelmed me.

He lifted his head and straightened his back. "Set it up with the producers while I sort out security. Tell them you'll be there in two hours. If they give you any shit about the short notice, let me know, and I'll take care of it."

With a stone-cold look settling over his face, Thomas became my professional bodyguard once again.

Over the next two hours, the physical distance he kept from me was just as notable.

"Katie, I'm coming in," Thomas said from the other side of the door.

"Yes, come in." I grabbed a sweater from the closet and met him in the center of my bedroom. "What's the plan? Will you be driving me and staying?"

"There're business matters my staff can't manage without me, and I can't put one of the meetings aside any longer. Carl will drive you and stay with you."

"Your driver, Carl, you mean?"

"He's quite capable, and I'll keep an eye on things."

Thomas was careful and thorough, and one hundred percent, I trusted him with my life. His tech skills were beyond comparison, so when he said he'd keep an eye on things, I could count on the fact that he literally had a visual surveillance plan.

As he escorted me to the parking garage, I noticed more cameras and the heightened security detail he'd hired to patrol the building.

Pausing for a moment before securing my seat belt and shutting me in the back of his Escalade, Thomas told me to be safe, and then he gave Carl a warning nod.

THE FILMING STUDIO WAS IN LOWER MANHATTAN, BUT with all the traffic, it might as well have been in Jersey. Even though we'd left in time to get home before dark, a nagging feeling sat heavily in my gut.

I didn't voice my thoughts, but Carl's instincts were spot-on.

"Don't worry," he said. "I know how to avoid some of this heavy traffic to get you back to Mr. Hastings before we lose daylight."

That was a relief. Something about this man gave me a sense of calm. He made turns unfamiliar to me, cutting through side streets and alleyways, taking us through parts of Manhattan I'd never been. I noticed stares as we passed a cluster of men who looked like they didn't appreciate our detour through their neighborhood.

"Never mind them, Miss Reed. They're admiring the car, is all."

Right. No one at a distance could see me through the dark tinted windows.

I dug into my bag for my phone, deciding to call Lena to see how she was doing, when I heard the crunch of metal and felt a jolt. It took a second to register that another car had hit us.

Carl cursed under his breath and turned on his blinker to show the other driver that he was pulling over. But the driver struck us again. And again. Each time with more force.

"Son of a bitch!" exclaimed Carl. "He's trying to run us off. Pardon my French."

"French all you want. He's coming around."

I peered out the window to see an old police car spray-painted black. It had a bull bar in the front and was swerving to gain access to our left. Carl gunned it, zigzagging to confuse our pursuer.

He was hot on our tail, skidding out as we made turn after turn to lose him. No sooner had we gained distance than he found us again, slamming the Escalade into a tail-spin. He rammed us into an intersection, sending us into oncoming traffic. Two small cars crunched into one another.

Carl expertly maneuvered the SUV out of the spin, slammed on the brakes, spun the steering wheel, and peeled out, barely clipping the front bumper of an older Buick. "Don't worry. They'll survive."

I was stunned, tossing my head to see the driver of the Buick jump out and curse us as our chaser sped through the wreckage.

"They'll survive? What about us?"

Carl glanced at me in the rearview mirror and tipped his chin. "Desert Storm. Special Ops. I've got you."

That explained a lot, but it didn't explain who this guy chasing us was, why he was chasing us, and how we were going to lose him.

"Don't be alarmed. I'm going to take him down an alley up ahead, slow down until he's right beside us, and run him into the wall, if necessary. Do you trust me?"

Did I have a choice?

"Don't answer that. Just hang on tight."

I gripped the armrests on my seat, my nails digging into the leather. As described, Carl took the turn, tires screeching as they burned against the street. Our tail was close to follow, but I supposed it was part of the plan.

"You see that fire escape up ahead?" Carl said calmly, as though he were pointing out the scenery. "If I time this right, he'll come alongside us, and I'll smash him into the wall right before we reach it."

I was about fifty percent confident that plan might work, but then again, I was trusting Carl simply based on Thomas's trust in him.

The Escalade slowed slightly, allowing the other car enough room to come around on our right. But the car came up on our left instead.

His window was down, and I saw a flash of metal before I screamed, "Gun!"

He pointed it right at me even though I knew he couldn't see me clearly. I ducked down, hunching over my lap with my hands over my head.

Shots were fired. One. Two. Three.

Red flashed through my psyche.

A screech and a crash behind us.

I opened my mouth, but I couldn't push out any sound.

fourteen

THOMAS

THREE HOURS AND FIFTY-FIVE MINUTES. I'D CHECKED THE time and the tracking app on my mobile so often that my client remarked on it before leaving my office.

Fuck him.

Katie's safety was my priority. She was working on a charitable project and having dinner with her collaborators at a filming studio in Lower Manhattan. I planned to pop in and see for myself that she was all right.

No evidence of the assassin's presence in the vicinity had turned up. I'd still taken precautions and set up safeguards. Studio management had agreed to lock down the building and call in the overnight security company. Along with other measures, I'd hacked into the city's camera system.

Carl had driven Katie and would stay with her. He was a capable man. A former sergeant in the US Army, he'd completed two tours in the Middle East and taken part in the raids at the Iraq-Jordan border during the Gulf War.

"I'll get the details sent out to legal and text you later with the time for tomorrow's conference call with the attorneys," Janie said. "Would you like me to copy Mr. Hastings?" My brother, she meant.

"Quite right. We'll keep him in the loop for now."

Will had started picking up the slack for me once I took Katie into my custody.

Setting down my cup of tea, I angled my wrist to see the time. The tracking app again. They were already moving, headed back to the Upper East Side. I quickly logged in to my penthouse security system.

Without looking up from my monitors, I said to Janie, "Post the Jensen files to the server once they've been updated. If anything else pops up and you judge it to be urgent, call me directly."

Janie agreed and excused herself.

Cameras covered the driveways out into the street, so I could see my car exit the garage on the recorded video surveillance as I reversed the footage. All points were secure. But right then, dread twisted in my gut. My instincts were innate and never wrong. My life and now Katie's depended on that.

Rewinding the video further, I revisited the time stamped thirty seconds before Katie and I had appeared in the garage. Carl waited by the Escalade. I closed Katie in. They had driven away. The Escalade came into view on the feeds, one by one as they passed each of the high-definition cameras. The images were clear. Nothing would slip by unnoticed.

Movement on another camera feed caught my eye. I'd put my attention on the Escalade as it had left the garage, but after setting the video back again, I focused on the surroundings.

I couldn't see where the fuck that bloody arsehole I'd hired to keep watch in the garage had been standing.

At the same moment Katie had climbed into the backseat of the Escalade, a man had been watching us from another location. I followed his movements, how he'd slipped through the shadows and waited in his car. When the Escalade had pulled out onto the street, the man had followed. I tracked him down the street until I ran out of surveillance.

Adrenaline rushed through me. I leaped out of the chair to open the wall safe where I kept one of my handguns. I had to get to Katie. Cut through the traffic. Get to her before he did. She was all that existed.

A racing pulse surged through me as I sprinted to the garage and sped off on my motorbike to catch the Escalade. They had a considerable head start, but on my bike, weaving through traffic gave me an advantage. The car finally came into view, spinning through an intersection, narrowly missing a pileup.

Carl maneuvered out of the intersection, and because he

then led his tail into an alleyway, I was certain he'd spotted me.

I sped up as the Escalade slowed. The other car braked and maneuvered round to the left side of the Escalade. It was too close. The fucking driver accelerated and gained on Katie's side, moving in on her window.

A flash of metal. The barrel of an assault rifle.

Anger and violence raged inside my soul as the bastard got closer to her. The training, my father's cruelty—I could finally channel it into something of worth. Katie's life.

Everything Will had done to protect Ellie took on a new meaning for me inside a transient moment. It was sacrifice. He'd taken a bullet meant for her. She was his life, and he would have nothing if she were gone. I finally truly understood their connection.

I drew my gun and shot three times. The first bullet shattered his rear window. The second disabled a tire. And the third …

I waited for his car to falter, and as I passed, I pointed my gun directly at his open window and pulled the trigger. Blood splattered. Not enough. I should stop. Finish the job. But sirens were already wailing, and Katie needed me.

I waved my arm for Carl to continue along the alleyway and followed until he pulled over in a quiet residential location. In seconds, I was off my bike and had the car door open.

Katie clung to my neck as I scooped her out of the seat and held her against my chest. I pressed my lips to her forehead while closing my eyes, forcing back the rage, confining it to the bottom of my soul.

I dropped my mouth close to her ear. "Do you hurt anywhere?"

She lifted her chin. Our eyes connected. A gray storm. No tears. "I'm not hurt. Thank God you're here."

I set Katie on her feet but couldn't let go, and she lay the side of her face on my chest. I willed my heartbeat to slow.

Always, I wanted to tell her. I would always be there. Always keep her safe.

Not yet. I couldn't say it aloud quite yet.

Instead, I nodded and placed a protective kiss on the top of her head.

She was lovely and brave. The truth was, she owned me. Admitting so was painful and beautiful. Like my heart had been brutally ripped from my chest, only to rest on a velvet cushion for Katie's pleasure and her pleasure alone.

"Nick of time, Mr. Hastings," Carl said, assessing the damage to the Escalade. "Did you take care of the aggressor?"

"He's wounded. I didn't get a direct hit."

Katie jerked her head up, touched my face. "Are you all right?"

The corner of my mouth twitched. A suppressed ego-driven smile. "I'm quite all right. Can you ride?

She nodded. I guided her to the bike and placed my helmet on her head.

Once seated, I said to Carl, "Clear out before authorities find you. Take the Escalade to the office garage. I'll send you a car."

WHEN KATIE AND I ENTERED THE PARKING GARAGE, I nodded at the security guard, now positioned properly and alert. Later, after Katie settled in, he would lose his post for the critical mistake he'd made. He'd be lucky to leave my employ alive.

Katie's knees buckled as she dismounted. I caught her, and she bent at the waist, twisting round in my arms to vomit.

Pulling back her hair while holding her in my other arm, I spoke softly to reassure her. "It's all right, baby. Let it out. I'm here."

Shock. I'd expected it once her mind had time to consider what had happened.

After finishing, she collapsed against me. I lifted her trembling body into my arms and carried her to the lift and then down the corridor to her bedroom.

Marta followed and fussed and even cursed at me, but I sent her away, making my position clear. She wasn't to enter the room without my permission. Not anymore.

Katie was mine, and I would take care of her.

"So cold," she whimpered as I put her down on the bed, her lips quivering.

"I'll get you warmed up." I removed her shoes and tucked her in beneath the quilt.

"Don't leave me. I don't want to be alone."

"I'm not leaving this room tonight, Katie. I promise." I took off my boots and climbed onto the bed, wrapped my arms round her, staying on top of the quilt, and pulled her back tightly against my body.

She'd no longer sleep alone. I would hold her every night and be her shield. Against fear, loneliness, the darkness of night. The truth was, I needed her just as much as she needed me. I needed to know she was safe. Needed to feel her warmth.

"Undress me, Thomas," she murmured, sliding my hand from her waist to her breast. "Please."

She wanted to make love. I understood that. A near-death experience could do that to a person.

No. There would be no kissing. No sex. I'd hurt her.

I took a deep breath and strengthened my embrace. "I won't touch you like a man touches a woman, Katie. But you'll not sleep alone as long as I'm near."

She turned round to face me, touched my cheek, held on to me tightly. "This is enough for now. But I do want more."

I kissed her forehead.

"Please see me, Thomas. I'm not a delicate little flower."

"I see you. And you're wrong. You're quite like a wildflower. Beautiful. Unexpected. Strong-willed."

What was more, she was my salvation.

She closed her eyes with a smile on her lips.

Before allowing myself to drift along with her, I stared at her sweet face, vowing silently to do everything in my power to deserve her …

And to find the motherfucker who had tried to hurt her and give him a slow, painful death.

fifteen

KATIE

THREE NIGHTS LATER, AND STILL, I COULDN'T REMEMBER the ride home on Thomas's motorcycle after the attack. He'd appeared at the car door and then carried me to my bed.

I remembered the mattress dipping from the weight of his body and then strong, warm arms, a lingering kiss on my forehead. The deep, rasping sound of his voice, the words like a sweet lullaby, but not like a child's cradlesong. They were a sensual serenade meant to be shared between lovers.

Thomas had promised not to leave me alone that evening. I'd pleaded with him to stay the following night and the next, and he had given in. I put on a brave face during the day, but when the nighttime came, I needed his reassuring presence.

The man Thomas had shot fled the scene, leaving

behind the unregistered car he'd used and no fingerprints, the news reports had said.

"I'll stay again, Katie. Understand, this is a temporary arrangement until I find the assassin," he warned. Then, he reminded me that he would keep his clothes on and sleep on top of the quilt. "Same rules. And wear proper pajamas."

In answer, I chose to wear as little as possible. A thin white tank top and pink pajama shorts. "These are my pajamas. This is what I wear."

After his eyes explored my body, he forced his gaze back to mine, pushed a hand through his hair, which was sexy as hell, and said, "You're deliberately making this difficult for me, goddamn it."

I shrugged and slipped into bed beneath the quilt. He wasn't wrong.

Thomas switched off the light and lay on his side. Forty-five seconds passed, twelve breaths. He cursed softly, "Bloody fucking hell."

Lifting my body and the quilt, he positioned me so that my back was to his front, and then he drew me into his arms.

"You're so lovely, Katie. You deserve to be free." His fingers were in my hair until he abruptly gripped my waist and yanked my backside tightly against his arousal. "Problem is, I'm quite a selfish prick."

Everything he did, all that he said—it was as sweet as it was infuriating, and it made me ache for more of his touch, for him to take from me what I knew he wanted, what we both wanted.

God, I needed for him to get past the guilt he carried. I was alone, locked inside an emotional cage, waiting for this man to free me. I'd saved myself for him.

"Be selfish, Thomas," I whispered. "If that's what it takes. Because I need you. I need you to remember us, the way we fell for each other, the park." His lips touched my neck. A chill ran through me. The good kind. "Please remember."

"I haven't forgotten." Warm breath against my skin. "Finding you changed everything for me."

"Then, why can't we be together?" I pushed my ass against him.

He grabbed my hips, holding me still while sucking hard where his lips rested. A reprimand. "If you do that again, I'll sleep in the chair. Now, go to sleep, Katie."

I squeezed my eyes shut to push back tears.

THE ABSENCE OF THOMAS'S WARM BODY BESIDE MINE WOKE me, the void leaving me anxious to feel the heat of his skin again. A sliver of light sliced through the bedroom from the bathroom door. I checked the clock. Four fifteen in the morning. Much too early. I waited. He was coming back soon. He always came back.

But when spray from the shower broke through the

silence, I couldn't stop myself from slipping out of bed and padding across the wood to stand before the door that separated us. I peered through the slight crack, wanting desperately to see him. With the heel of my palm, I gave a light push, knowing the door would slowly fall open on its own.

Thomas was naked, steam surrounding his powerful body. Hot water rinsing away the soap from his magnificent chest, pouring down his chiseled ab muscles, rushing lower, running over his hard penis.

I swallowed, my throat tight and dry. I wasn't sure what I'd expected, but everything about this man was overwhelmingly big.

He wrapped a hand around his thick length and pumped angrily. Grunts came from deep in his chest as he stroked, eyes squeezed shut, as if he were still sleeping, still dreaming.

Mesmerized, I was rooted in place, watching him. It was the most sensual thing I'd ever seen. I pretended he was using my body instead of his own hand, and a blooming sensation shot through me. I licked my lips, wishing I were in the shower with him, our bodies pressed against the tiles, his enormous erection inside me …

Thomas's eyes opened, and I gasped. I should have known. His awareness was unrivaled. A flash of erotic danger was in his gaze as it met mine. His expression warned me not to approach the glass, but I was not going to obey. Not while his eyes held mine as he still stroked himself, his fingers sliding from base to tip.

More steam settled on the glass, blurring his image. I stepped closer.

"Go back to bed, Katie." His voice was throaty, shaky, like he was too breathless to issue commands in his usual way.

Desire washed over me, a delicious ache between my legs. I wanted to rush under the water with him and let him touch me, fill me, relieve the want inside me. The feeling was so strong that it hurt. I placed my fingertips on the glass, dying to be closer to him.

His eyes shut again as a breathy groan escaped him. "Katie, go. I can't stop."

He didn't stop. He rested his tattooed forearm against the wall and dropped his head onto it. He thrust his hips, and the muscles on his ass and thighs strained as he pumped into his hand, slamming into the pleasure, his body shuddering as he came.

His shoulders caved as he panted, working to slow his breath, the shower stream cascading over his muscled back. He turned his gaze to me, not at all surprised to see me still watching him. "You shouldn't have come in here."

There was no chance I'd walk away now that I'd seen how it could be with him.

"I want to be with you. Don't send me away, Thomas. Please," I begged.

He straightened his back, and after staring at me for ten seconds, he slid open the glass and offered me his hand.

"Keep your pajamas on," he ordered, the strength in his voice returning.

I gave him my hand and stepped in, the water soaking my clothing and my hair at once. The thin fabric of my tank top clung to my breasts, presenting my erect nipples to him. His throat rumbled in response.

In an abrupt move, he captured my wrists and covered my mouth with his, thrusting his tongue inside. He pushed me against the tiles, still kissing me fiercely, releasing my arms, only to hold me in place with his hips as he cupped my breast and grabbed a fistful of my hair.

Breathless, panting, starving for more. My lips sought his again, my tongue matching his, stroke for stroke.

I reached for him, but he caught my wrists again, gathering them into one hand and raising my arms above my head, not allowing me to touch him.

His eyes dropped to my chest and moved lower, his free hand reclaiming my breast. He dragged his thumb over my nipple, sending an arousing shock through me.

"I want you," I said, remembering how he'd thrust his manhood into his fist. It scared me and thrilled me. I wanted him to do it to me. "I want you to be inside me." I tugged to break free of his hold.

"Stop it," he growled.

But I didn't want to stop. I ached for him. There was no coming back from that kind of need.

"Thomas," I moaned, lifting onto my toes to meet his

touch, begging him to use his thumb again. I twisted my arms, my hands.

"I said, stop." Darkness flashed in his eyes as he increased the pressure on my wrists. "You will obey me, Katie."

"But I—"

"You nothing," he snapped. His pupils dilated, constricted, his emotion alternating between pleasure and anger. "Do you see me, Katie … the way I see you? Look closely." Another part of his soul revealed itself in his eyes —the savage intensity he'd kept from me. "I'm a fucked up bastard. You want me, and that pleases me, but the cost is more than I'll allow you to pay."

Something unexpected raced through me. My vision narrowed. The rapid pounding of my heart sped faster. He'd made me angry. "I'll decide what I'm willing to pay and for what. *That* is the only freedom you owe me."

Our eyes were locked. Neither of us moved a muscle. Five seconds. Ten. Fifteen seconds.

One corner of his mouth twitched and then curved into a smirk. He pushed the lower half of his body against mine and then pulled back. "Look what you've done."

My gaze dipped to his erection, glistening with droplets of water. The sight wasn't unpleasant, as Lena had described, not to me. I found it masculine, stunning, inviting.

"I'm ready," I said, challenging him, pleading with my eyes and my small voice.

The stream of water pounded on the shower floor, echoing off the tiles, and his giant, looming form made me feel tiny. But I raised my chin and held his blue eyes with a piercing stare.

He let go of my wrists but remained close, caging me inside his heat. “Have you ever had an orgasm, Katie?”

Blood rushed to my cheeks. I would never admit it to anyone else, but after watching him pleasure himself, I wasn’t ashamed to tell him. “Yes, I have.”

His face changed, a lightning storm raged in his eyes, and he clenched his fists at his sides. “How? With whom?” He said the words through his teeth, demanding details.

A possessive hand landed on my hip, his fingers pressing into my skin, as if to say, *Your orgasms are mine*. It was the truth. He was the only man I’d ever wanted.

Fury surged in his voice, and he pushed for an answer. “You will tell me now.”

“Fingers,” I blurted. “Mine.”

His grip relaxed, jealousy receding from his eyes. His gaze then swept over me with adoration and lust. “Masturbation doesn’t count, baby.”

The term of endearment, combined with the deep timbre of his voice, sent bolts of electricity through my veins. Every nerve ending in my body was on high alert.

“Your first is mine. Spread your legs.”

It was happening. He had no intention of losing what was his.

Thomas put my back to the tiles, commanding me to do

as he'd ordered, and used his knee to open my legs wider. He ran his fingers along the elastic of my sleep shorts, teasing me, tugging at the fabric.

"You'll surrender to me. My name will be the only thing you remember. You'll cry it aloud when you come. But only after you've begged me, writhing in sweet agony, will I allow it." He kissed me, nipping at my bottom lip as he pushed his hand into my shorts.

As he dragged his fingers from my entrance to my clit, the world spun with vivid color, no numbers, no math.

"Christ, you're already quite wet," he said, his voice gravelly.

With one fluid motion, he plunged a finger inside me, making me gasp with surprise and ecstasy. He slid his finger in and out, testing my capacity. He slid out for a moment, returning again with two fingers.

"Oh my God," I moaned, hardly able to form words.

Is this what it would be like to have him inside me?

I'd pleasured myself before, but never like this. I'd never ventured lower than my clit.

"This is mine," he growled into my ear, tugging on the lobe with his teeth.

"Yes," I replied huskily. It was all I could manage.

He smirked as he trailed hot kisses along my jaw, down my neck, making circles with his thumb while his fingers moved in and out.

My orgasm was building like a tsunami wave rushing to

shore. I reached out for him, desperate to find purchase. So desperate.

"Stay put," he commanded. "No hands."

I was free-falling out of control. I needed to dig my fingers into his skin. I wanted to scratch and clench and flex. Pleasure coursed through my body, rising, rising. But then he slowed, killing me with want as he withheld my release.

I was on the edge of a cliff, begging him to let me fly. "Don't stop. Thomas, please."

He kissed me, teasing me with his tongue, sliding his fingers out of me, taking away the warmth of his hand. He moved my body so that my back was in the corner. "Hands above your shoulders."

I obeyed, raising my arms, my knuckles resting against the tiles on either side of my head. "Take me," I pleaded.

Thomas kissed my neck, sucking as he moved his mouth down, pausing to tug on my nipple with his teeth, biting through the clinging fabric. Taking his time, sending me to the brink, he lowered onto his knees, kissing my stomach as he tugged down my shorts, and then ordered me to step out of them once they hit the shower floor.

Placing my leg over his shoulder, he buried his face between my thighs, kissing gently at first, bringing the orgasm closer again. His tongue ran along my seam, propelling me into the stratosphere. I couldn't take it. It was coming on too fast. He licked and tasted, parted my folds with a groan, and plunged his tongue inside while thumbing circles over my clit again. And then he replaced his thumb with his tongue, pressing hard, circling, pressing, his fingers inside me again.

It was a heaven I'd never experienced. I squeezed my eyes shut, and stars formed behind my lids. I was falling through space, floating weightless into oblivion. I might have died as my climax rose higher and washed over me in a delicious rush, my body convulsing.

"Thomas," I cried. No other words, only his name existed for me, just as he'd warned.

He stood and gathered me in his arms as my knees failed. "That's right, baby. You belong to me."

Giving me a minute to catch my breath, he kissed my temple, my forehead, the tip of my nose. Then, as though I weighed nothing at all, he swept me up and carried me to bed.

Amazingly spent, I didn't register him removing my wet top or wrapping me up inside the quilt. His arms were just there, so strong, holding me, his warm breath on my neck. My mind and my body drifted into a heavy lull.

When the sunshine woke me, the last thing I could recall was his soft promise.

"I'll be back soon, Katie. I will always come back."

sixteen

THOMAS

A TORMENTING SURGE OF GUILT STRUCK ME LIKE A SEVERE punch to the gut. I swallowed hard, shut my eyes tightly for a minute. Neither action relieved the discomfort.

"What is it, Thom? You look like you're in pain." My younger brother, John.

He and Evans had arrived at the penthouse before dawn. Before I went in to shower.

I had sworn not to touch Katie, not like that, not yet. She had pushed me, parading about in her so-called pajamas, rubbing her arse against my cock, asking me to recount the time we'd spent together. None of it excused my behavior. She wasn't to blame.

I'd never managed impulse control and restraint properly. Discipline had largely been imposed upon me by my brothers rather than by my own self-compliance. I meant to change that and grow the fuck up. I'd done well enough … until Katie.

The way she wanted me, begged me. My ego had—and would again—refused to let it go unanswered. But something stronger than even my ego gave rise to my transgression. Though she wasn't aware of the mark she'd made on me, she had indeed changed me. Her pure soul had reached into mine, claiming parts of me that I'd never given another woman, compelling me to give her everything she wanted. Never mind the consequences. She owned me.

Katie had wanted to join me in the shower, and I'd been obligated to give in.

Christ, I had no idea how to manage our situation, moving forward. I had no plans to live without her, though she needed time on her own first. My position on waiting hadn't changed, but I'd messed up by inviting her into the shower, further complicating matters. Because now that I had tasted her, watched her orgasm from my touch, there would be no instance in which I could deny either of us the physical intimacy we desired.

There was no help for the reality we faced. I fancied Katie's beautiful mind, but I also craved her body, needed to thrust into her tight, wet cunt. The ache was bone deep. And my determined little love would drive me straight to it.

"It's nothing," I told John. "I'm quite well."

I turned my wrist for the time. Five fifteen. Twenty minutes before sunrise.

"Listen, you don't have to keep things low-key round

me, brother. I understand why I'm here. I mean, you've been in and out of her room several times in the two hours since we've been here."

"It's complicated. We'll leave it at that until I return." I raked a hand through my wet hair and gulped down more coffee. "Grab Evans while I ring Will, and let's finish up here. I need to get on with this lead before the trail goes cold."

I need to be gone before she wakes.

No good-bye. Katie would question what was happening and give me shit for leaving.

Will answered on the first ring, expecting to hear from me. "John's all right?"

"He is. And the family? I'm putting you on speaker."

"Everyone is well. Ellie, Lissie, the babies. Mum is worrying over John, of course. Anything new from the reconnaissance team this morning?"

"The gunman is injured, but he's not going to stay put for long."

I'd put a bullet in his neck.

After the confrontation, Will had met with the director general. Director Martin called in support from two MI5 assets in the States. The men gathered intel on the prime minister's assassin, the details mined primarily from a US military physician who'd turned coat and gone rogue. He'd treated the hit man's wound. He'd also been amenable to the intel team's bribe, offering up the exact coordinates of the safe house where he'd left the assassin to convalesce.

Our allies still had eyes on him, and we'd scheduled the attack for midnight.

"Keep the hit clean. Don't overstay your welcome. Understand me when I say, it will cause her more harm than good if you fail to quickly purge the aftermath and return to her. Leave that shit behind with the body, Thomas. She'll help you with the rest."

I shook my head. "The situation isn't the same for us."

"You're consenting adults. Her consent was legal even at seventeen, and I'm quite certain you know that. This fucking heroism of yours isn't sustainable, and it can only cause heartache. Christ, Thomas, we're not heroes. We don't allow ourselves to be enslaved by any one situation. Who you are and whom you love can't be changed. Learn from my mistakes. Do what you must to make Katie happy."

Speaking with my brother was often like tapping into my subconscious. I already knew what he wasn't afraid to say.

The time would come when I'd be ready to switch gears, moving heaven and hell and destroying any obstacle to have her. She was mature and clever, which made her age a subjective barrier that wouldn't stop me in the end.

"Your advice means quite a lot to me—you know that," I said.

"But?"

John entered the room and interrupted, gripping my shoulder as he moved round me to claim the position on my right. A Hastings move. “Have you told Ellie that I’m here with Thom now?” he asked Will. “She wanted me to check in right away. Threatened to kick my arse over it.”

“She’s sleeping late this morning. I’ll tell her the moment she opens her eyes,” Will teased.

As they talked, I stared at John. Katie was only two months younger, but there was a remarkable difference between them when it came to their life experiences. My brother had traveled. He’d seen death and horror. He could defend himself and her. Kill if necessary. And he’d been out of the house, allowed to explore and discover on his own.

Katie was innocent, kind and caring, trusting, and being with me might change it all. Those were the stakes, and I’d lay them before her when I came back. I wanted her to know. I wanted to show her and make her choose me again.

“Contact me at once if you need anything at all, Thomas. And, John, keep me posted while he’s out,” our older brother said, and then he disconnected.

Once I was confident John and Andrew fully understood my commands, I packed up the laptop I’d prepared for the mission and grabbed my jacket and helmet. I flew out of the garage, heading for my flat, where Carl waited for me with a car.

I was completely focused, my instincts vigilant and my reflex response primed, as should be the case for any man pursuing vengeance. Taking care of this motherfucker was personal. He'd tried to hurt my woman, and now, his life belonged to me.

MARTIN'S AGENTS HAD THE TARGET ON-SITE BY THE TIME I arrived at the safe house. I instructed them to wait outside in their van. No one was to enter the old farmhouse, not until I exited and the governor's cleanup crew finished.

The moment I stepped inside and entered the same room as the assassin, rage began to boil. It was a madness that took over my mind and allowed the other man to rise from my soul—the killer who'd been trained by his father to end life, the beast who would kill to defend Katie. It would consume me.

"You've been informed. You know my name and why I'm here," I said, stepping into the light.

The prime minister's assassin sat on a wood dining chair, military-grade paracord wrapped round his body, his wrists, his ankles. A thick cloth gag silenced his voice. He let out a muffled curse.

"Let me be clear. You'll die with or without telling me what I want to know. Your words really aren't that valuable to me. I can get the same intel from multiple sources. Should you speak when I allow it, doing so will not save your life. Saying shit that I don't want to hear will prolong your suffering."

Yanking at the cloth, pulling it down over his chin, I

noted the bandage on his neck. Another few centimeters, and my bullet would've taken him out.

The motherfucker spat at me. His eyes darted about, looking round the empty room, sizing me up, searching for my weapons. "Fuck you," he snarled. A threatening sneer. He was underestimating me.

"Good. You do understand," I said, striking a blow to the side of his head. Blood ran from his ear. "I don't intend to use weapons this time, as you can see."

My brothers and I had trained as hand-to-hand combat fighters from the age of twelve, and we preferred to use our fists when punishing those who had tried to harm our family, our women.

The contracted assassins used by the British government were skilled sharpshooters, often lacking military combat training. The look of this one confirmed in my mind that it was the case in his instance as well. He'd trained with guns, not his body.

I walked round and stood behind him. If he spat at me a second time, I might kill him too quickly. "Tell me what Reed has on the prime minister."

He was quiet. Motionless.

I struck the back side of the chair with my foot, sending him onto his face. I retrieved a knife from the one table in the room and then cut the rope on the chair.

"Nothing to say then." Kicking the chair away from his body, I ground my boot against the wound on his neck.

An agonized howl. Blood pouring from the wound, pooling on the wood floor.

"I'm given a target when contracted, not a reason. You know this," he rattled.

"Fair enough." I bent and cut the ropes binding his wrists and his legs. "Get onto your feet."

He didn't move. "Get on with it and kill me, you fucking worthless imitation of your brother."

Madness. Fury. I was nothing more.

Using his hair, I jerked up his head and snarled in his ear, "You will get the fuck up." My hands were there before me, gripping on to him, his clothing, yanking his body upright.

A sharp blow to his right kidney. Another. One to the left.

Tortured cries. Panting. Wheezing.

He caught himself on the wall, hands frantic for purchase, his fingers digging into the crumbling plaster. "Put a bullet in my head, motherfucker. Do your job. Kill me," he slurred, begging for leniency.

My fist drove into the center of his back, and he slid to the floor. I kicked him, turning him over. He would see my face when he took his last breath. I positioned myself over him, towering above, my feet on either side of his body.

The bastard was quiet again before closing his eyes, tears streaming down his face. "This … it's about the girl."

I dropped to my knees and roared, "No one comes after what is mine."

As I pounded into his flesh, breaking bones, spilling more blood, he cried out incoherently, his words once again seeking mercy but receiving none. "I thought it was Reed. Didn't want to hurt her. The blonde hair. I saw her. Another will follow. Use her to flush him out."

My mind, my soul, both owned by rage.

Bloody, broken fists. My chest heaving.

No more words. No breath. He was beyond recognition. Eyes staring at me. Gone.

I'd beaten him to death.

I squeezed my own eyes shut.

My brother's voice carried above the violent chaos in my head. "*Purge ... return.*" His reminder. Leave my sick hell behind with the body. Will knew. He'd taught me quite a long time ago how to cage the darkness.

"She'll help," I said aloud.

I looked down at myself, searching, searching through the red, moving my gaze over my shirt, my skin. There. There it was, the little bird on my forearm.

Pushing up from my knees, I stood and straightened fully, breath still pumping angrily through my nostrils. Three steps to the left, I pulled on the dangling string and put out the bulb. There was no light then—no moonlight, no lamplight, nothing penetrating the thick black draperies.

I closed my eyes once more and pulled an image of Katie's face into my mind. She was the peace that I'd found, the only peace I might ever know. A lovely light, burning brightly in the darkness, waiting to show me the way out.

The sound of breath rushing in and out of my chest climbed, rising into my throat, hissing through my ears. Slowing, softening, becoming my silence.

I needed to get back to Katie. Keep her safe. Allow her to warm my cold blood.

Not yet. I needed time to be certain the rage was locked down before seeing her.

Bloodthirst and anger had retreated, but shades of guilt remained. It wasn't black or white. Guilt was my gray. It held me captive in the goddamn space between depravity and morality, selfishness and self-sacrifice, to condemn me for the lives I'd taken.

It tormented my heart, punishing me for everything I was about to take away from Katie.

Still, I would take what I wanted from her.

I'd just killed a man for her, and there was no coming back from that.

seventeen

KATIE

THOMAS WAS GONE. IN HIS PLACE, TWO STRANGERS HAD assumed command of my home.

Of course, I had expected them to arrive eventually, but seeing Andrew Evans in the hallway, pacing between my room and the foyer, still startled me. I stopped dead in my tracks.

A military-looking rifle hung from a strap hooked over his shoulder. Muscled biceps stretched the sleeves of his black T-shirt. The pants he wore and the boots also suggested a military vibe. A colorful dragon rose from his collarbone onto his neck, its gaping mouth breathing fire below his right ear.

He quickly disconnected from a phone call and raised his right hand in the air, as if to wave hello to me. "I'm Andrew Evans." He extended his hand, offering to shake mine. "Forgive me for alarming you, Miss Reed."

I stepped forward and accepted his handshake. "No, I'm sorry for pulling the stupid face. Thomas doesn't wear anything like that, so it was a surprise. Please call me Katherine—no, call me Katie."

"You all right, Katherine?" John Hastings entered the foyer, coming from the dining room.

Holy shit.

His eyes. The way he carried himself. He was a true likeness of Thomas. Smaller though. Shorter.

I nodded. "I'm fine. Thanks. I was just telling Mr. Evans I'd like to be called Katie."

John grinned. "I'm not sure my brother would like that. I think we'll stick with Katherine for now."

Even the way his mouth curves reminds me of him.

"Come with me to the kitchen for breakfast." He turned his wrist, his familiar eyes darting to his watch. Then, eyes skipping back to mine, he extended that hand to me.

The number eight. Dominance, strength. A deep sapphire color appeared in my mind. John's masculine presence mocked the feminine undertones. Even his scent was distinctly masculine. My brain didn't hesitate for a zeptosecond to assign the same numeric identity as it had given his brother.

All the Hastings brothers must share it, I thought.

I put my hand in his and allowed him to lead me to the kitchen. "Do you—I mean, are you into mathematics, like Thomas?"

"No, not at all." He started removing items from a large

brown sack. Food and coffee from Jack's. "He's the only genius in the family. I play football."

"Thomas mentioned you were playing for Loughborough University. I imagine they'll want you back soon for training." I sipped from the tall paper cup he'd handed me. My coconut milk latte. "Thank you for coming over to help your brother."

John swallowed a mouthful of toast, dipped into the runny yolk of a fried egg. "You don't need to thank me, Katherine. This is what we do, my brothers and I. Thomas would and has done the same. Family comes first. Always." When he reached across the island counter for his cup, ink identical to Thomas's stretched out from under his T-shirt sleeve.

I missed Thomas, his tattoos, the strength he gave me, his kiss. My heart ached to be near him. A quiver ran along my spine, my body recalling his touch, his teeth pulling on my nipples, the thrill of his tongue between my thighs. A quick breath caught in my throat.

John tugged on his sleeve to reveal the entire shield. A lion. Roses. The Latin word *Defensor.* "It once represented an old protection pact between two families, but that's quite a long story. I'll let Thomas explain. What's important is, in the present, it symbolizes our commitment to our own family, our promise to defend it at all costs."

I nodded. I understood their desire to keep their loved ones safe, understood Thomas's obligation to investigate my father. It didn't scare me or make me want him any less.

He wouldn't find anything on my father—nothing criminal anyway.

"He didn't tell me why he was leaving or when he'd be back."

"Trust me, my brother will be back. Give him a day, maybe two."

"I think I know what he's doing. He went after the assassin."

"Quite right. I don't think he meant to keep it from you. Not really. Seeing you in more distress would have affected his mood, messed with the clearheaded focus necessary for him to complete the mission." He pointed to my scrambled eggs with his knife. "Eat."

I took a bite of scrambled egg. Chewed. Swallowed. What the hell was it with these Hastings men? It was a compulsion to obey their commands. "I'm not in distress, you know. And I'm not a child."

"No, we aren't children, Katherine." He set down his cup. "You remind me of my sister-in-law."

"Ellie, you mean. She's a countess, right?"

"Yeah, she doesn't like to be called by the title though. It annoys her. She was an American as well. But it's your spirit I'm talking about. You're fierce about your independence, but it's balanced suitably."

Narrowing my eyes, I said, "Explain what you mean by 'balanced suitably.'"

"It wasn't an insult, but rather the opposite. Ellie would tell you the same. My brothers and I are like alpha wolves, she says. It's in our blood; it can't be changed. You might think that makes strong women a poor match." John shook his head as he nailed me with his stare. "Truth is, the challenge is a requirement to satisfy us, to keep us from boredom, and to keep us in line."

"That's really intuitive. And brave to say. Can I ask you something personal—"

An alarm sounded. John sprinted to the dining room. I followed.

As he studied the security monitors, he communicated with Andrew. "Where the fuck are you? I have an alarm set off and a garage camera out."

I heard Andrew's response through the speaker on John's phone.

"Stay with your charge. I'm standing before that camera now. It was hit with something. When it blacked out, I came down the emergency stairwell. Inspect windows and doors and lock down the lift. Go. Quickly. I've got you in my ear. Let me know what you see."

John grabbed my hand, his grip harsh and unrelenting. He gave no instruction, said nothing to me as he pulled me along. "At the lift now, locking it down," he told Andrew. Then, he turned to me. "You must keep your back against the wall in every room while I check things."

The sound of my heartbeat rushed through my ears. I stared at his face.

"Katherine." He squeezed harder on my hand. "Got it?"

"Okay, yes," I breathed.

“Kitchen first. Come with me,” he ordered, moving, towing me behind him.

John gripped my shoulders, positioning my back against the one solid wall in the kitchen. I watched him inspect the locks on the terrace door, the windows.

Gripping my hand again, he pulled me into Marta’s room. One window. Locked.

Hallway. The library.

“Back against the wall, Katherine,” he barked.

The living room. My back to the wall.

Hallway. The stairwell Andrew had used.

My parents’ suite. Against another wall. Terrace door. Windows.

When we entered my bedroom suite, the terrace door was open, the sheers blowing in and out.

John drew a handgun from his belt. “Did you leave this door open?”

I shook my head. I couldn’t remember. Thomas had ordered me to keep it locked.

“Katherine,” he shouted at me. “Did you open that door?”

Did I open it? “I don’t know. I … I don’t know.”

He kicked open the closet, making sure it was clear.

“Wait, please,” I cried, fumbling for the switch to the light fixture as John pushed me through the opening.

“You do not come out until you see my face again, Katherine.” He shut the door. “Evans, the exterior door in her bedroom is wide open.”

"I'm almost there, John. Do you have a visual?"

"Negative."

A loud thud. The terrace door. It was the sound it made when hitting the interior wall.

My breath quickened. I braced myself, fingers tightly gripping the back of my dressing chair. My mind refused to count the breaths. *How many were there? How fucking many?* I'd always counted them when the thunderstorms scared me. When my father was gone. I'd hated him for it.

"Thomas, please come back," I whispered.

Rumbling voices cut through the long silence. Andrew's and John's.

The walk-in door opened, and I flew into John's arms.

"It's all right. Everything is okay," he told me. "No one is inside. We've got this."

I lifted my head from his shoulder and locked on to his eyes. The contact was unsettling. He was too much like Thomas.

I pushed away from him, straightened my posture, and nodded. "So, it's safe."

Andrew nodded as well. "Yes. More security guards arrived. We've cleared the building."

"I'm so sorry if it was me. I didn't mean to cause any trouble."

"Katherine, if you did, it doesn't matter. That wouldn't explain the unanticipated movement within the garage." John grinned. "No more going out onto the terrace. Deal?"

Five hundred twelve. Eight to the power of three. Three wolves. Sapphire waves.

I sighed then, relieved to have my brain working properly again. "Yes, you have a deal."

"Shall we finish our breakfast?"

"I don't think so. Not now. But thanks for getting it in. I'd like to call my mother."

He handed me his phone. "Ring her on mine. I don't want communication between the two of you traced right now. Not until I hear from my brother." Tilting his head toward the door for Andrew's benefit, he added, "We'll give you some privacy."

"Um, no, I'll go into the living room, if that's okay."

John dipped his chin, understanding my reluctance to stay alone in my room. "Yeah, of course. I'll be close, just in the dining room." He motioned for me to walk ahead of him.

"Thanks." I followed behind Andrew, tapping my mother's number into John's phone, aware of both men, their boots on the wood floorboards, covering ten more feet of hallway to the next room.

"Mom," I said as she picked up. "Thomas is gone. Don't worry. I'm not alone. His brother and a soldier are here along with the extra security guards he hired. Did you know about this?"

"Sweetheart, hello. He did inform me of his plan. How are you holding up?"

I swallowed hard. “I would be a lot better if my damn parents were here with me.”

I heard her speaking to someone, asking them to give her a minute. A moment of silence lingered while she waited, and then she let out a weighted sigh. “I am sorry for that. He ordered me to stay in Albany. It was part of the deal. Do you think I want to be away from you while this situation is ongoing?”

A nervous laugh escaped me. “Situation? Oh my God, Mom. I was nearly killed, and your husband is being pursued. Or are you so busy that you’ve forgotten us? But you know what? Thank goodness for Thomas because he certainly hasn’t forgotten about me. Even if he did order you to stay there, it’s not like you and Dad were ever home anyway.”

Emotion twisted inside me, making my hands shake. I was growing angrier with her, resenting her for what she’d done to our family. For her absence.

“Katherine, please, just settle down. I get that you’re upset with me. And maybe you have that right, but speaking this way won’t solve anything. What worries me even more is the attachment I’m sensing on your side of this, darling. Thomas is not the kind of man with whom you should get involved. He’s a trained killer, and he won’t think twice about shedding another man’s blood.”

“You don’t even know him. Not the way I do.”

“Oh, but I do. I know so many men like him. You are to keep your distance. Do you understand me, Katherine?”

"Too late, Mom," I taunted. "Zero distance."

"Do you know where he is right now? He's hunting down the man who attacked you. To kill him. Do you understand what that means, darling? He will return to the penthouse soon after killing another man."

Confusion. Fear. Emptiness. Tears threatened to spill, but I wouldn't let them, not when I needed to prove to my mother that I, too, was a strong woman. She had never seen that in me.

An angry surge overwhelmed me again. "Stay out of my business, Governor, and I'll stay out of yours."

"Katherine! I don't know what's gotten into you, but you will not speak to me that way. A man like Thomas Hastings has a dark soul. Whatever kind of crush you might have—"

"I don't care. How are his actions any different than yours? He protects his family, as we all do. You. Me. Dad. There's no difference. If you believe Thomas is a monster, then aren't you one as well for what you've done? You might as well have killed *him*."

She fell silent—a rare moment for Carolyn Reed. The truth was that my family had ugly secrets. I wasn't ready to unveil them for Thomas. The secrets weren't mine to tell. Not only that, but I was also confident he would uncover them himself, which would keep me from betraying my family.

I realized then why he'd been pushing me away. He saw me as faultless, pure. But I wasn't. I was a liar with secrets that I wouldn't share with him. I wanted desperately to tell him, to make him see that I understood his position, that I could live with the things he'd done.

That I loved him.

But I couldn't tell him any of it, not yet. I needed to work things out further.

I knew in my heart that he would go back to London soon. It was his home. His brothers were there. Would he want me if we were both in the UK? Would it be easier for him?

I'd accepted the offer from Oxford.

Mom broke her silence. "That hurts, Katherine. There are things you don't understand. You're still so young."

"I don't mean to hurt you. Please, Mom, put yourself in my position. I'm an adult, like it or not. I grew up faster than you care to admit. I've been surrounded by professors and politicians my whole life. I'm not as naive as you want to believe. I'm ready to move on … and I'm going to Oxford."

"What? No, honey. You're angry and confused right now. That's all. We'll work through it."

I closed my eyes. I didn't know what I was feeling right then, but it was no longer anger. "No, I'm not. And I'm sorry for the way I spoke to you. I love you and Dad so much. Still, I've never been more certain about anything. I am going to London."

"I won't accept this. Not at all, Katherine."

"I hope you will someday," I said softly. "I really do."

She didn't say anything else. Words left unsaid hung in the air between us, but speaking them wouldn't do either of us any good. I heard as her assistant entered her office, and they discussed an appointment.

Then, she said to me, "Don't do anything yet, darling. We'll talk through it this evening. I'll call you as soon as things quiet down here."

Immediately after hanging up, I searched for flights to London, buying myself a one-way ticket.

I knew my mother. She would cut off my credit cards to punish me if I didn't give in. But that was okay. Let her. Oxford's fellowship was fully funded, and I could easily wait tables or make coffee to earn extra cash.

I was Katie Reed. Freedom was mine, and I refused to let anyone take it away from me.

eighteen
THOMAS

STRIDING OUT OF THE LIFT INTO THE PENTHOUSE FLAT, I hurried down the corridor to Katie's bedroom suite, dismissing Andrew Evans from her personal security detail with an abrupt nod while brushing past him.

"I'll stay on the monitors. Ring if you need me," he said with a hint of commiseration in his tone. He understood the darkness that clouded a man's soul after he'd taken another life, how it changed him, what it took for a man to move beyond it.

I would thank him later.

Getting back to Katie was my priority.

I stepped inside her dark bedroom and locked us in, staying near the entrance.

The fucking curtains were open.

She was standing in front of the French glass doors,

peering out at the sky, watching the stars shine, as she often did when she was too restless to sleep.

That was what she had become to me. The stars. Every single last one of them.

"Katie," I said, my tone low, unintentionally guttural.

One word—the name she'd given me at the coffeehouse. A name that hadn't been her name at all, although now, it belonged to me. The sound of it, the sense that it was all mine, made my cock twitch.

In response to my voice, a sharp inhale. "You were gone," she then half-whispered, gripping the white-painted doorframe, leaning into the sheer draperies.

City lights illuminated her white nightdress, outlining the shape of her curves beneath it.

"I'm here now."

"I don't want the others here. I trust you."

"You can trust my brother. I wouldn't have gone otherwise." I wanted to cross the room and pull her into my arms to reassure her that she would always be safe. Tell her that I would never let her down. I wanted to kiss her mouth, touch her body.

"Why are you here now, tonight?" she demanded.

"I gave you my word that I'd come back."

"You'll leave again."

"I should go now."

"Go then, Thomas. Get the hell out of my room."

She'd spoken softly, but the tension in her body projected anger. Good. That was good. I wanted her to be furious with me. It was the least of what I deserved for what I'd done to her before leaving, for the hunger boiling in my blood in that moment.

"If that's what you want."

I'll do anything for you, even when it hurts. Even if it kills me.

Her forehead touched the glass, her face reflecting on the pane. Closed eyes, long lashes touching her cheeks, lush pink lips. "I want you to stay. I want more from you."

"Be certain, Katie. Understand what that means."

While Katie was lost in her thoughts for a moment, quietly, I prowled to the center of the room.

Her eyes opened wide, staring out at me from the glass, and her back straightened. "I'm not sure I do understand," she said, lying.

The pretty lie on her lips only strengthened my desire to have her in my bed, to control her.

She was many things, but never a fool. She knew how her challenge would affect me, that I was a selfish prick, yearning to take everything from her.

I accepted her invitation. "Remove your clothing, Katie. Keep your eyes on the stars."

Slowly, she pushed the nightdress off her shoulders and let it fall to the floor, pooling round her feet. She stepped out of her knickers.

"Good girl. Show me how you pleasure yourself."

Katie slid a hand down the front of her body, pausing to feel her pebbled nipple. Her head dropped back, and long blonde locks fell onto her arse, touching what was mine. Her breath quickened. Moaning, breathy, she slid her other hand between her thighs as well.

Christ, she hadn't hesitated to indulge me.

My cock grew harder, kicking out for her as I watched. I was desperate to bury myself inside her, to have her warm body writhing beneath mine.

Unable to stay away any longer, I ended the physical distance between us, moving in close behind her. "Stop touching yourself, Katie."

"Please, no," she breathed, full of desire and need, her hair tumbling against my chest.

I captured her hands and pulled them to her chest. "Katie," I warned, stroking her nipples with the back of my thumbs while holding her wrists, my lips on her neck. "You'll do as I tell you."

"Thomas, please. I need—"

"You'll give yourself over to me when we're together this way. You will obey me." I pulled the fingers she'd used on herself into my mouth and sucked on them. Sweet, salty, addictive. One taste wasn't enough. More. I wanted, needed more of her. Needed her to heal me. "Say it," I ordered.

Katie relaxed, allowing her body to fall against mine. "I'll obey you."

I rewarded her trust by releasing her other wrist and caressing her curves. She shivered, goose bumps rising on her soft skin wherever my fingers touched her. I kissed her neck, licked it, tasting more of her, and then tugged on the rim of her ear with my teeth. Lowering my palm, pressing it against her clit, I pushed my forefinger into her, and she drew in a sharp breath.

"I want to do things to you too," she said hoarsely.

Another finger. "Close your eyes and feel me."

She moaned. "I want to go down on you, the way you did to me in the shower."

Fuuuck.

My cock pulsed, as if her mouth were my home.

I bit her shoulder. "Careful, little bird." My fingers moved inside her little cunt. So tight. I would destroy her. "What you're asking me for might not be as you imagine."

"Oh God … Thomas …" Whimpering, she turned her head, offering me her mouth.

Her orgasm was coming on quickly. Watching her luscious lips form a circle, her nails digging into my flesh—it was making me mad with desire. I wanted to throw her on the bed and fuck her until she couldn't walk, live inside her velvet softness, feel her orgasm clenching round me.

She would be perfection.

I was too worked up. I would hurt her.

As my fingers moved in and out, my thumb caressing her clit, I kissed her.

"Thomas," she cried onto my lips, reaching her climax.

"Mine, baby. They're all mine now."

Her body trembled as she let go, trusting me to keep her safe in my arms while she remained in the orgasm. I held her, kissed her, gave her time to catch her breath. Her breasts rose and fell, slowing, slowing. She twisted in my arms to face me, and I pushed into her mouth with my tongue.

Our tender, deliberate kiss changed, becoming my confession. It was rough, merciless, my mouth devouring hers, taking over, taking everything, conveying to her the way that I would love her.

After I broke the kiss, her gaze searched mine. I wanted to fall into the loveliness of her eyes. Moonlight poured over her features, giving her an ethereal appearance. A beautiful, mystical creature, imprisoned in the arms of a selfish beast.

Katie smiled. A playful, inviting smile that made me want more, compelled me to lose my shit.

My craving for her consumed me. I wouldn't take her, not yet. But that mouth. She wanted to blow me.

I grabbed a fistful of her hair. "Unzip my trousers."

She obeyed, taking her time with the button, sliding down the zipper, running her fingertips below the waistband, dragging them over my skin. Quite innocently, she smiled up at me from beneath her lashes, unaware of the fire her fingers ignited within me. How it tortured me.

"On your knees," I growled.

"I've never done this."

"I'm going to teach you. Down."

Katie lowered onto her knees, one at a time, holding my gaze, and pulled on my jeans. Her eyes widened as my hard length fell into her hand, thick and heavy.

I wrapped my hand round hers, guiding her long, hot fingers, slowly sliding our hands together. She tracked the motion with her eyes for a moment and then pushed my hand away. My good little student.

"Come closer."

She leaned in. I captured her other hand and showed her how I wanted her to handle my bollocks.

She explored me on her own then, cupping, stroking, and pumping.

I let her go, groaning, my hands in her hair. *Christ.*

She was already doing quite well. More. Always, I wanted to take more from her.

I brought my hands round to cradle her face. "Now, kiss me."

Ease her into it. Go slow with her, just this once.

Before I could give another command, her lips touched the head of my cock while she continued pumping with her fist, and then her little pink tongue swiped across and swirled through the droplets of pre-cum. My breath caught. I hissed.

"Show me your eyes, Katie."

She looked up. Swirling. Licking. Killing me. Pride in her stormy-gray eyes. A rumble in my chest climbed to my throat. She would be the end of me.

"Take me into your mouth."

Alarm flickered in her features.

It was quite a lot for her to take into her mouth. But I was too far gone to let her off the hook.

My hands in her hair, I tugged. "You won't disappoint me. Now, finish what you started."

Katie's eyes lit with an innocent curiosity, with trust. The words, my command, had given her confidence. She licked her lips and then opened wide.

Fuuck. Me.

I pushed into her beautiful, plump circle. She tightened her lips, wrapping velvet heat round my cock, and I breathed her name. She tightened more, making me mad with want. I pushed in deeper, pulled back, in again, knotting fistfuls of her hair.

She let out a moan as she took over the motion, sucking, sending me over the edge. Her hand pumping. Tightly sealed lips. The mind-blowing friction from her hot tongue.

The first jolt of orgasm hit me. "Ah Katie. You're killing me."

I couldn't hold back any longer. Keeping her head still, I rocked into her mouth, fucking it with desperate thrusts. I pushed in and out of her sweet mouth, pumping harder and faster than I should have, using jerky primal movements.

She took me into her throat, tears welling in her eyes, and held on to the base of my erection with one hand, clinging to my leg with the other.

The climax rushed through me, throwing my body into delicious spasms, filling her throat. For a fleeting moment, I reached an altered state of consciousness, and my mind began healing, cleansing my soul of the blood I'd spilled for her.

While catching my breath, I looked down. Katie's hands were on my thighs. She'd swallowed down quite a lot, but a bit had spilled onto her chin. I pulled her up from the floor, wiped it away with my thumb, drew her against me.

"I've been harsh with you. I'm sorry, Katie."

"No, I liked it." She wrapped her arms round my torso, the side of her face resting on my chest. Then, she asked quietly, "Was mine as good for you as the others?"

"What? Goddamn it, Katie." I caught hold of her chin and pulled her face up, so I could see her eyes. "Don't do that. Don't make comparisons. No one has ever made me feel as good as you do." I sucked hard on her bottom lip to punish her.

She bit mine as I released her and then pulled back with a smile. "Ever?"

I grinned for a second, pleased with her courage. "Yeah. But don't ask me about that kind of shit again. Instead, you look at me, see me, feel me." After kissing her lips softly, I pressed her face back to my chest, her ear positioned over my pounding heart. "Hear me."

Christ, I'd never spoken that way before.

I loved her.

Truly.

nineteen

KATIE

I ROLLED OVER IN MY BED AND PROPPED MYSELF UP ON AN elbow. Thomas was there, not a dream, lying on his back, one arm thrown above his head. His eyes were still closed, and his bare chest rose and fell in a perfect pattern. Even in his sleep, he was gorgeous. Long lashes. Full bottom lip. A masculine jawline, beautifully angled and covered with a three-day scruffy beard.

When he'd returned the night before, he'd been altered. He hadn't said the words, but the raw pain in his voice and in his eyes had told me what I wanted to know. He used physical intimacy to heal his emotional wounds. I could give him that, could help him come back from his darkness with my body. And I had.

But he hadn't been the only one in pain. My father's life was in danger, my family on the verge of shattering. And Thomas had left me when he could have stayed, believing the job had to fall on him, though he had men working for him who could do the same.

I'd been angry with him, but it hadn't lasted long. Because I'd missed him too damn much.

Lena had asked the day before if knowing Thomas hunted another man to kill him scared me. It didn't. Thomas's upbringing had created that part of him. I knew his heart, and it was generous and loyal and even tender when he allowed himself to feel connected to me.

My fingertips were drawn to his face like magnets. I reached out but quickly thought twice. He was under the sheet with me for the first time, and I didn't want to wake him and ruin it. The quilt lay in a heap on the floor. I didn't need it. His body heat was more than enough to keep me warm.

His body. I lifted the sheet and peeked beneath it. Low-cut pajama pants and—

Thomas's hand captured mine, surprising me. I sucked in a sharp breath. He pulled my fingers to his mouth, kissing my knuckles.

"Only for you, baby." He opened his eyes and winked, and we smiled together.

"Do you mean your erection or the pajamas?"

A tangle of hair dropped onto my face. He pushed it away. "Both."

I smiled again. "We can do this, you know."

He lurched upright, his feet hit the floor, and he

dropped his face into his hands, as if my words had hurt him.

I watched quietly, stunned, waiting for him to say something.

"We have here and now. There can't be anything more for us. When this is over, when I know you are safe, I'm going back to England."

No, please, not yet. It was too soon. Tears stung the back of my lids. "But what about Hastings Group? You were just saying how much you needed to get done."

Neither of us had been able to sleep, each of us wanting more of the other, so after pushing him and losing, we'd talked into the early morning hours. About his company. His family. He revealed there was a second assassin. Asked me why I wasn't upset with him for investigating my father, for potentially apprehending and delivering him to the British government.

"I can only say that I'm confident my father is innocent of any crime against the prime minister. You won't find him guilty of espionage, so there's no reason for me to be upset with you. You'll do your job, and in the end, you'll actually clear his name, so he can come home," I had told him.

My answer hadn't satisfied Thomas, but he'd promised not to pressure me, as he had when we first met at Jack's.

"Katie, you know I've hired an operations manager. It's quite easy for me to work remotely. I'll fly in to see clients when necessary."

More stinging. A lump in my throat. I longed to confide in him. To share the secrets that weren't mine to tell. To tell him that I'd accepted Oxford's offer and I would also be going to England. So much was at stake. We'd made progress in our relationship, gaining ground, only to find ourselves at the beginning once again.

We would fail irrevocably if we built our relationship on secrets and lies. I knew this. But for now, I would keep my plans quiet and pray that he could work through his self-inflicted guilt trip.

"You swore your reluctance wasn't about my age. That you truly wanted me, wanted to do the right thing for me. Well, here I am, telling you what I want and what's right for me, that I want you too."

His hand dropped from the top of his head, and he twisted his body to look at me. "Katie, Christ. I haven't lied to you about any of this. You need to take time to find your dream and live it. Then, when you're happy, if you still feel quite the same, I'll be here."

The tears fell, and there was no stopping them. I closed my eyes. "A dream isn't worth much if there's no one to share the thrill and the joy of it."

"Don't cry. Please. The miles must separate me from you so that I can't hurt you."

Fury rushed through my blood. More tears. My life. My choices. My pain. I didn't know how to make him see that he was hurting me now.

"Get. Out. And this time, I do mean it."

He stared at me. I threw a pillow at his face. He instinctively blocked it, making me even angrier.

I pointed to the door. "Get the fuck out!"

THOMAS SPENT THE FOLLOWING HOURS ALONE IN THE library, doors closed, his voice rumbling through the walls as he barked orders by phone to his employees at Hastings Group, security team, and informants.

Before leaving my room, he'd made it a point to show me that he was still the one in control. "This is quite good, Katie," he'd said, stopping at the door for a moment. "You're angry with me, as you should be. For what I've done already. For what I'll take from you when the time is right."

I had thrown another pillow but too late. It had struck the door, and then I'd shouted that he was such an asshole.

"Show me more, Katherine," John ordered, interrupting my thoughts.

Lucky guy. He'd won the lottery. Thomas had assigned monitor duty to Andrew, but John's task was much worse. He was to babysit the grumpy little bitch that his brother had offended.

I shook my head and began erasing my whiteboard wall. "I'm sick of looking at this stupid wall. Call me when you're back at Loughborough. I'll give you more calculus cheats when you need them." Without a breath, erasing and obliterating the first column in a week's worth of work, I continued, "Is Carl back yet? Hey, can we get something to eat? When is Thomas coming out of the damn library? God, now, I know what it's like to need a drink."

"Slow down, girl. Christ, breathe. And no drinking. Thom's orders."

I stopped erasing and pulled a face while mocking his words. "*Thom's orders*."

John heard me. "Come on now. He means well."

I spun on him. "That might be true, but I'm not currently following his orders."

Every fiber of my being wanted to obey Thomas, but I wasn't ready to let him win. He would always win, and I understood that about him. Even so, I couldn't keep my mouth shut either. I'd done it all my life with my parents. No more.

To make matters worse, Lena was temporarily out of the picture, and I needed to confide in someone. "Can you keep a secret, John? For me, please, just for a few days. A week, tops. I really need to talk through something."

"I'm here for my brother, but I'm now your friend as well. So, yeah. You can trust me—as long as it doesn't hurt my brother."

I smiled. "Thanks. It won't. And I think I'll tell him soon anyway."

"Go on then. You have my word. Let's hear it."

"It'll be easier for me if my brain has something to process."

I held up the eraser. He nodded. As I moved to the next column and reviewed what remained of my work, I made mental check marks, dragged the eraser over the black markings, and moved to the next equation. Repeat. Repeat.

"I've accepted an offer from Oxford. I'm going to London. Honestly? It's likely that I won't come back here to live after completing the fellowship. It would be nice to have a friend there when I arrived."

Erase. Repeat.

"Quite right. I'll show you round the city."

Side-glance. He was smiling. Repeat.

"That's generous. Thank you. No one else knows at this point, so please, keep it between us for now. John, I'm so sorry for behaving poorly. That's not like me. I've always been accommodating. It's Thomas, I think. He has changed me."

"Our brother Will says that's what happens. You find the one, and you both change a little. Thom needs the challenge." He chuckled. "Anyway, I've given you my word, and you can count on it. But I am concerned that you'll need help, getting started in London, Katherine. Even just knowing which pubs are safe for you is quite important. For meals, I mean."

I laughed, touched by his kindness and by his loyalty to Thomas. "Maybe an occasional cocktail with those meals. You know, the wine fridge in the kitchen is fully stocked."

Just like that, my banished bodyguard appeared, his huge form consuming the entire doorway. It was like he had superhuman skills that detected the moment my plans didn't meet his approval.

I stopped erasing, dropped down from my tiptoes, turned to meet his eyes. He said nothing aloud, but his hot gaze dived to my toes and prowled up my body. A similar experience to the one I'd had during our first encounter at Jack's slammed into me. With his icy-blue stare, he influenced my feelings, commanded my behavior, stirred a primal urge inside me.

Savage.

I wanted him to put those savage hands on me, his mouth, the erection pushing against his jeans.

He broke the silence, the sound of his deep voice finishing me off, making my panties wet. "Meet me at the lift at seven. And, Katie, you'll wear this dress for me."

Two white boxes with black satin ribbons were tucked under his arm. He set them on the chair just inside the door, and then he walked away.

twenty
THOMAS

LELAND JENSEN HAD REQUESTED A DINNER MEETING. HE appreciated my staff, he'd said, but he preferred to get to know me on a more personal level. His wife had made reservations at an exclusive Michelin-starred restaurant in Tribeca.

Jensen was quite right. The business relationship between us required assurances. As an angel investor, he supplied capital to fund the production of an electric-car prototype owned by another of my clients. The fees I charged for managing the capital were significant, and I wanted to get him on board for a second project. I needed to present him with the opportunity before leaving New York.

I'd replied to his email, accepting the invite for three. I didn't want Katie out of my reach, not even for a few hours. She was safer with me. John would join us and maintain comms with Evans.

My contacts hadn't yet produced intel on the other assassin, and I had no plans to lie to Katie about it. She needed to understand the seriousness of the threats against her life.

I checked the time. Ten minutes.

Buttoned my shirt, tucked it into my trousers. Cuffed the sleeves. Nine minutes.

Though we were in the same penthouse, I hadn't seen Katie for hours, not since taking the dress to her room. I couldn't wait to see it on her body, and then after an evening of anticipation and torment, I would strip it away. I had confidence that I'd selected the perfect dress, that later, she would allow me to remove it from her flawless body.

I'd hurt her.

I poured two fingers of scotch and let the burn slide down the back of my throat. She'd been quite angry. Furious, ordering me away. It had taken everything in me to tell her that I was leaving, that I'd put an end date on us.

My words had crushed her, destroyed the loveliness in her eyes, wrecked her beautiful optimism.

"We can do this," she'd said.

My Katie. Her smile had nearly killed me. I'd desperately wanted to agree with her, to take her into my arms and give her what she wanted. But instead, I'd left her in tears like some fucking stranger off the street.

I pinched the bridge of my nose, contemplating how

much more shit she might take and questioning if she would even come back to me. If I were to let her go.

Can't do it. She's mine.

John abruptly pushed into the library. "Thom, you ready? I've got Evans in my ear on comms. We inspected both cars and briefed Carl. We'll stay behind your SUV in Reed's."

"Has she come out of her room?"

"Not yet. A guard's on the monitors. I'm going down to the garage."

I gave a nod, and he turned to leave.

"John … I'm glad you're here."

A side-glance over his shoulder. "Me too, brother."

As I headed for the lift, I stopped myself from checking the time. It didn't matter. She was worth every second, and waiting for her was something I needed to learn to live with anyway.

Katie's bedroom door opened. The staccato clicking of the Tom Ford stilettos I'd given her was hypnotic. I rubbed my chin, eyes locked on the woman coming into view. Christ, the sway of her hips, the way the dress clung to them, to her breasts, the hem brushing over the top of her thighs.

My cock came to full attention as I devoured her with my eyes. To see her in something I'd chosen for her body was quite a rush.

Nude-colored tulle, the boutique owner had said before sending it and the shoes over. Floral beading and embroidery, wildflower petals fashioned from clear, ruby, and sapphire crystals.

Katie stopped six feet away and held my gaze with hers for a moment. Her berry-stained lips curved into a subtle smile. "This … is a ten-thousand-dollar Oscar de la Renta."

Eyes exploring, I took in her loveliness. "The price tag is nothing. Seeing it on you is everything."

"It's an amazing dress. Thank you, Thomas. I forgot my bag. Give me a minute to grab it." Slowly, she turned and walked down the corridor to her room.

She'd calculated the move. And thank Christ she had because there was nothing on the planet more exquisite than her arse in that dress. If she'd ordered me onto my knees right then, I would have fallen to the floor straightaway.

Over her shoulder, she tossed a seductive little smile at me.

No way was I waiting for her to come back. As soon as Katie hit the threshold, I snatched her wrists, pinned her against the wall, and spread her legs apart with my knee, pushing myself against her stomach. A gasp came from her pretty mouth, reminding me how well she'd blown me the night before.

I growled close to her ear, "Don't fucking tease me."

She waited for my eyes to return to hers, lifted her chin. "My virginity is yours. Just take it, and I'll stop. Please."

Losing it, I clutched her hair in my fists and jerked her to my lips, kissed her hard, thrusting my tongue in and out of her mouth, biting her. To reprimand her, to show her how rough it would be with me.

She accepted the punishment and pushed me for more, rubbing her hot tongue against mine, dragging her hand down to grasp on to my pulsing erection.

Intense need shuddered through my body. I groaned. I pulled back, releasing her mouth, and stared into her gray eyes while she worked to catch her breath. "*You're* mine, Katie."

It was she who was ruining me.

She nodded, still calming herself.

Because I was a prick, I slid my hand up her thigh, pushed the piece of lace aside, and drove my finger in and out of her wet little cunt. She hissed, moaned, said my name.

"You'll stop trying to seduce me, or you'll get nothing." I removed my hand. "Understand?"

Disbelief filled her eyes. "Why would you do that and then just stop?"

I raised a brow, not needing to explain.

Katie nodded with awareness. "But it'll happen?"

"It will. Quite right."

"I trust you."

"Good girl. Now, let's go to dinner." I'd caged her in with my body, with my influence, and it killed me to set her free. A soft kiss on her lips, and then I backed away. Pain sliced through the center of my chest. I put my hand on the soft, bare skin on the small of her back. Touching her eased my discomfort. "Come. We'll be late as it is."

ATERA HAD BEEN A BRILLIANT RESTAURANT CHOICE. IT WAS a twenty-course tasting room, intimate and elegant, seating no more than sixteen guests in one evening.

Evans and Carl remained outside on security detail. John had joined us for dinner, holding his position on Katie's left while entertaining her and Sandra Jensen.

In the car, she'd asked me not to introduce her as Katherine. I had no issue with it. I wanted her to be comfortable and happy. Nothing else mattered.

Katie had wrapped the Jensens round her little finger by the time we reached the dessert courses, captivating them with her genius and her beauty.

Sandra placed her napkin on the table, grabbed her wineglass. "One of those universities will be so lucky to have you, Katie. Have you accepted an offer?"

"I'll need to make plans soon. I'd like to go where the strongest prospect exists for me to make a difference." Katie set down her glass of champagne. I'd allowed her two. "I'm interested in community engagement. I support change in the educational systems that hold children with learning disabilities at a disadvantage. The disabilities often go undiagnosed, and the kids are commonly disciplined for poor performances and behavior. Those same children would excel with proper teaching methods."

I broke from my conversation with Leland and pulled Katie into my side. She had dodged the question, asserting her right to choose the life she wanted even though her mother had set things in motion at Columbia.

"Katie recently collaborated with professors at Columbia to design a mathematics program for children with dyslexia." I kissed her temple, reached for my glass.

She looked up at me with something in her eyes so lovely, something I'd never experienced, something for which I couldn't find the words.

Then, she leaned in, rising close to my ear, and said, "Thank you, Thomas."

The Jensens announced their departure and said their good-byes. Katie and I waited for John to check in with Evans and text me with an all-clear before I took her out onto the street.

She'd thanked me again. I hadn't responded because I wanted her alone first.

When the lift doors closed us in, I pulled her chin up and kissed her lips. "You don't owe me any gratitude, baby, not now, not ever. There's nothing I won't do for you. But listen. Don't mistake my actions for gallant gestures. They serve my own needs. I'm not a good man."

"Stop saying things like that, Thomas." She kept her voice low and soft, her eyes on mine. "What you've done tonight is worth more to me than I can say. You freed me, if only for an evening. That's something only a good man would do."

Christ, she never stopped surprising me. I didn't know what I'd do without her.

I pushed a lock of hair behind her ear, cradled her face in my hands, kissed her again. "You're my everything, Katie. I can't lose you. Forgive me for hurting you this morning."

She smiled. "I forgave you hours ago."

"The dress?" I teased with a wink.

"Of course not. This dress means something to me because it was a gift from you. You could give me rags, and I'd love them. It was your brother. John helped me see what had happened with more clarity."

I smiled, pressed my lips to her forehead. "My brothers are quite skilled at saving my arse."

The lift doors opened. I extended my arm in front of her and stepped out to scan the lobby.

Another young couple heading out. Three middle-aged women. Two men. A security guard, a female employee, and a male employee, all standing near a central desk. Four cameras. Three sets of doors, one revolving. John, crossing the lobby, heading outside to the car.

I reached back into the lift box for Katie's hand. She stepped out beside me but then stopped.

"Move quickly, Katie. We must get to the car," I told her, sliding my hand onto her back.

Color drained from her face. She screamed.

I lunged in front of her to shield her while scanning the lobby again for threats.

The couple. Three women. Two men. Security guard. Female employee.

Carl. Evans with his weapon drawn.

My brother, lying on the ground, a knife in his back.

twenty-one

KATIE

I TUGGED AT THE HEMLINE OF MY DRESS, ONE OF OSCAR DE la Renta's runway beauties. A mid-thigh, crystal-embellished masterpiece. Embroidered flowers, their leaves and vining stems covering my body. I'd seen it featured in *Vogue*'s spring layout. Even my mother wouldn't have been able to get her hands on the wildflower dress, but somehow, Thomas had managed it.

Trauma did strange things to the brain. Mine used the dress to keep me present, to help me hold on for Thomas's sake. He needed me, needed me to be strong for him and for his brother.

Something wet and cold dripped onto my thigh. I let go of the hem, looked at my hand.

John's blood.

Thomas was on his knees, beside me, telling his brother to hang on, to be strong, that he would be okay. I told him to move his hands back to the knife's handle again. Thomas gripped the top with his other hand while I quickly slipped mine under the one with which he held the blade. I applied pressure on the towel surrounding the blade. My hands were smaller, a better fit to secure the blade at the point where it'd entered the flesh.

John lost consciousness. "From the pain, the shock," Carl said.

Andrew hovered above with a gun, his head turning, turning, watching our backs.

Blue beading. Ruby crystals. Sapphire. Sparkling white. Thomas's face. His smile. His horror. No numbers. No goddamn numbers. Why? Where has that part of me gone? My heartbeat quickened. *Nude tulle. A halter neckline. An open back.*

"John, come on, brother. Open your eyes," Thomas ordered.

Sirens screamed through the streets. Flashing red and blue emergency lights pierced the glass and spun around on the interior walls. The paramedics had arrived. Three men and one woman rushed in. The woman instructed us on moving our hands, so she could take hold of the blade and wrap it.

We got on our feet, and I staggered backward, bumping into Andrew. His arm snaked around my waist to catch me. I righted myself and watched Thomas cradle John's head in the palms of his hands while the paramedics lifted his brother onto the wheeled stretcher.

"Is someone riding along with him?" the woman medic shouted.

"Where is she?" I heard John say.

Thank God. He'd come back to us.

"Katie's safe with me," Thomas said. "We're coming with you."

John turned his head as much as he could to see me. The medics had strapped him to the stretcher, immobilizing him to keep the blade stable until surgeons could safely remove it.

"You take her home, Thom. Evans can ride along."

I stepped up to the stretcher, touched John's cheek. "We're not leaving you. I'm fine. Thomas won't let anything else happen to either of us."

Thomas held up his finger in answer to the medic's repeated question. "She's quite right. I've got you both. Now, be still, John."

John gave a slight nod, and then he closed his eyes as the medics rolled him out.

We arrived at the hospital twelve minutes later. The trauma team took John to the operating room at once. Carl and Andrew had stayed behind to speak with police and get the cars home. It wasn't long before they joined us at the hospital.

Thomas's heart pounded heavily as he held me against his chest, his strong, warm arms like a cocoon. We stood that way, waiting in the surgery corridor for word from the physicians. My feet ached, having worn the stilettos for hours, but Thomas was comforted by our position, and I wouldn't take that away from him. I held on to him, my arms wrapped tightly around his torso.

When we spoke, we spoke softly without letting go.

"Was it the assassin?" I asked.

He kissed the top of my head. "No, it was not."

"How do you know?"

"The incident was quite slipshod. But it must be related."

I lifted my head to see his eyes. "What makes you think so?"

"I feel it in my gut. My instinct is never wrong. Maybe one of his mates gone rogue. A male employee was missing from the lobby just after John went down. That isn't a coincidence."

A set of steel doors burst open, startling us. Three doctors pushed through.

"Mr. Hastings," one said. "We have good news. Your brother will be fine. The blade got caught up in the cartilage between his second and third ribs. The attacker didn't have the momentum or the strength to penetrate it. John's a healthy young man, and he'll heal nicely. He'll need time off from anything strenuous."

Thomas pushed his hand through his hair and let out a heavy breath. "Thank you. That's quite good news. How much downtime? He plays football for Loughborough University."

"One rib is cracked. It's not misaligned, so we believe

it'll mend properly over the next six to eight weeks. Once fully healed, it shouldn't affect his game. He only needs to manage the pain. Some patients will alter their breathing to avoid the pain. If John does this, get him to rehab for breathing exercises. We don't want him damaging his perfectly good lungs. I'd like him to rest here tonight."

"Money's not a problem. Give him whatever he needs. Thank you," Thomas said, shaking hands with each doctor.

I held on to his arm, rubbing his biceps, as we made our way to the recovery room. Thomas conducted a visual inspection of his brother, kissed him on the forehead, and then stepped out of the room to call Will, their older brother.

John and I chatted about his mother, his sister-in-law, and his niece, Lissie. The morphine then kicked in, putting him to sleep. God, he didn't deserve to be there. He was an amazing guy, kind, always concerned about his family. I couldn't imagine losing him. He'd become such a good friend to me.

I looked over my shoulder to see Thomas no longer on his phone. He stared into the room from the opposite side of the glass, his body like stone, his eyes moving back and forth between John and me.

It was my fault his brother was lying in a hospital bed.

THOMAS PLACED A HAND ON MY BACK AS HE ESCORTED ME to the car. He was alert and businesslike. A cold, distant mood had settled between us.

One step forward, two steps back. Addition and subtraction—the simplest forms of math.

We'd had a breakthrough. I'd found a better understanding of the way he was behaving, the guilt he was drowning in and why it existed in his heart.

But just as I'd begun to get a handle on it, he seemed to be letting it go. He asked me to forgive him—or rather he ordered—admitted he didn't want to lose me, and then he told me I was his everything. As he was mine now.

He finally saw what I'd been trying to show him all along—that he'd freed my soul. In that moment, there was a shift in him. Our step forward. A glance at a future together.

Only minutes later, we'd lost our momentum, sliding backward, losing ground again. John had been attacked, and I was the reason for it. I could see the emotional chaos in Thomas's eyes, the way he had stared into the hospital room. He wanted to blame me as well.

There were two things I understood clearly about Thomas Hastings. For one, I was in love with him. And two, he loved his brothers so much that he would die for them.

When we reached the car, I turned to him before getting into the back. "I'm so sorry. Leave me at the penthouse with guards from now on. Please, I won't argue when you need to go."

He stared at me for five seconds, six, seven. "You're tired, Katie. Get into the car." His words were soft, his breath warm on my cheek, but he broke eye contact too quickly.

I nodded, salty tears building up, burning.

Guilt had found its way between us again. But now, the guilt belonged to me.

Our car arrived in front of my father's building, and Carl let us out at the lobby entrance. Andrew rode down to the parking garage with Carl. Thomas had instructed the two men to pop in on the security guards, conduct a full-scale building check, and use the private stairwell entrance to the penthouse. Carl had stepped up to help with security detail.

We exited the elevator, and Thomas locked it down at once. "Take off your shoes. You'll stay with me while I'm inspecting the rooms."

But before I had the chance, he crouched and removed them for me. Then, he ran his hand up my leg, under the hem, to my inner thigh. His blue eyes burned into mine with white-hot fire. He kissed me there. His lips, his tongue, moving heat through him onto my body, boiling my blood, sending it all to my core. With one kiss, he set me on fire, took my breath away.

I slipped my fingers into his hair. "Thomas, what are you doing? You're upset with me."

A fleeting moment of confusion flashed over his face. He stood, gripped my waist. "What you see is concern for my brother." A soft kiss on my lips. A tug on my hand. Back to business.

He led me through the apartment and surveyed the windows and doors. We entered my bedroom last. The terrace doors were secure, the draperies closed. No words. Neither of us spoke.

Thomas slowly peeled off my dress, every movement agonizingly slow, his hot mouth on my shoulder, my neck. "So beautiful," he whispered against my skin.

I shivered.

"Beyond exquisite."

"Thank you," I whispered back. "I can say it when you say something like that."

He nodded his agreement—a compromise—and dragged his lips to my ear. "You'll stay in this room until I tell you otherwise."

My breath rushed out. "Stay with me."

Thomas stepped back, his eyes raking over my bare body.

"Get some rest, Katie."

twenty-two

THOMAS

Early the next morning, Carolyn Reed burst into the entrance gallery. Evans had caught her arrival on the monitors and sent me a text in warning. He greeted her and ordered her guards to stay near the lift to wait for further instruction.

"Yes, I think that's probably a good idea," she told him, nodding at the two men from her detail. "Where is Mr. Hastings? I'd like to meet with him in private before I see my daughter."

Evans didn't have time to respond.

I shut the bedroom door behind me and headed for the gallery. "Governor, we'll talk in the library."

Carl handed me a cup of coffee as I passed by the dining room.

"Thanks, mate. John will be ready this afternoon. Katie and I will come out through the lobby at twelve thirty."

Carolyn followed behind quietly, turned on the light, and closed us in. When she turned, she nailed me with a cold stare. "Your hair is wet."

"That's correct. I just showered. Why are you in the city without discussing it with me first?"

"You forget yourself, Mr. Hastings. This is my apartment. My city. And my daughter's name is Katherine."

"Cut the act. We had a deal."

She narrowed her eyes. "Sleeping in Katherine's room wasn't part of the deal. What is with men like you, always taking what doesn't belong to you? Tell me, I'd like to know if my daughter is still a virgin. Or have you taken her virginity as well?"

I took a drink, set the cup down. "Men like me keep people like you alive. We teach your daughters about predators and how to defend themselves—"

She scoffed, sparking my anger.

"You haven't taken time to teach your daughter a thing, though it's not quite about time. It's a heart you lack, Governor. To be clear, it's none of your business, but I'll answer your question to spare Katie the pain of doing so. Her virginity is intact." I rubbed my chin. I owned it, as she'd said, and craved taking it like a motherfucker. Not sure I'd hold out much longer. "It is today anyway."

"If you touch my daughter, I promise you I'll—"

"You'll do nothing." I stepped close to her, irritated, looming. "We were seeing each other before you came to me for help. I agreed for her sake, not yours, because I already cared for her. When you see her—if I allow it—you'll see that she does belong to me. She won't even have to say it."

Carolyn shook her head, her icy mask falling away. "Please, you must let her go. Your lifestyle, what you do—she's naive about these things. She won't understand it. Katherine is a special young woman who needs to be guided properly."

I'd intimidated her. Not what I'd wanted, but her attempt to threaten me had complicated the situation.

I moved round the desk to give her some space. "You haven't guided her. Christ, you've locked her away. If she's naive at all, you're to blame."

Her gaze fell to the floor for a split second. "Does she know about the assassin … and all the others before him?"

"Yes. Look, we both know what your next move will be, so I'll speed things along. There's an age difference. We're aware. We've talked about it. Katie's not a child, and she knows her own mind." I crossed my arms against my chest.

"Do you love her?" Carolyn asked softly.

"Do you?"

"What kind of question is that? Yes, of course I love my daughter. Name your price."

"There isn't a fucking price. We're done here." I checked the time. "You have one hour to spend with Katie. Then, I want you out of the city. I've sent your guards outside. I don't want anyone near her that I haven't vetted myself."

My mobile buzzed with a text alert from Evans. I read the message as I walked away from Carolyn.

"Her name is Katherine," she said to my back. "I wonder, did she tell you that she's leaving? She purchased an airline ticket, you know."

My heart dropped into my gut.

She wasn't lying, the spiteful bitch.

"One hour, Governor. Ticktock."

Evans waited for me in the dining room. He'd captured two dark images moving through the garage while reviewing the overnight footage. Three forty in the morning. The back of a man's head. White shirt. Black jacket. Another shadowy figure appeared within camera range at five a.m.

"It's the same man." I pointed out the lower angle on the second image. "You can tell by the way he moves. The shirt collar is clear in both clips as well. Open the file with the tenant information."

Chris Reed owned the building, and we had immediate access to his records.

"Well, this is interesting. One of the units listed is vacant. 4-C." Evans slid his chair over to the monitor with the live garage feeds. "But 4-C's parking space has been occupied all week."

"Give me the plate number." I entered it into my system, and NYPD's database quickly returned a hit. "The car was reported stolen three days ago by a woman on Long Island."

I scraped a hand over my face. Thoughts of Katie overwhelmed me. I'd stripped her out of that dress and kissed her shoulders, her neck, her lips. My coarse stubble had marked up her delicate skin. I missed her. I'd worked through the night. Too much shit was falling through the cracks, even with Will picking up the slack.

Sometime before dawn, I'd climbed into bed to hold Katie. Without opening her eyes, she instinctively snuggled into my arms. She'd been sleeping still when her mother arrived.

"What do you want to do?" Evans asked.

"Disable the tires. We'll watch closely and grab him when he surfaces again."

I STOOD NEAR THE WINDOW, SPEAKING TO MY CONTRACT lawyers, when Carolyn Reed entered the dining room. Her usual stoic expression ruined her otherwise attractive face.

Only forty-five minutes had passed.

"Mr. Hastings, I would like to leave. Thank you for taking care of my daughter." She hesitated for a moment, softened. "Please, Thomas, advise her against her plans. I wasn't able to convince her myself."

Fuck. I needed to see Katie. She'd lied to me again.

I nodded at Carl and then turned my back to quickly finish my business conversation.

Carl's chair scraped over the wood. "Ma'am, I'll escort you to your security team."

When I found Katie a few minutes later, she was at her whiteboard, using a mathematics conjecture to distract herself, as she likely did when something bothered her. She didn't stop. Her eyes stayed on the board.

Look at me. Feel me.

The marker fell from her hand, and her chin dropped. "My mother told you."

"You've been lying to me again."

"I planned to tell you tonight."

"Tell me now."

"I accepted Oxford's offer when you were gone."

Breath rushed out of my lungs at once. I'd had no intention of letting her go, and it no longer troubled me to admit it. She was mine, and I would follow her anywhere necessary.

"Katie, look at me."

She turned, nailed me with stormy, determined eyes.

"The choice was yours to make. You want to travel, and England is quite a good start. It's also my home."

Tears abruptly filled her eyes. "I know you don't want me there, but—"

Her fucked up words triggered me. I lurched forward and confined her against the wall, fixing my hands on either side of her head, restraining her body with mine. I dropped my head, hovered over her ear with my mouth.

"Have I not made myself clear?" I growled. "I want you there, here, everywhere."

"Show me. Do more than just undress me." Her eyes burned into mine while she pushed against my hard cock. "I needed you last night."

"My absence wasn't because of you, Katie."

"Maybe, maybe not. But you left me again to go and live alone in your dark place."

"You know what I am."

"Yes. I'm not afraid." She softened the timbre of her voice and searched my eyes. "I know that I'm safe with you in the physical sense. But how can I feel safe in this relationship if you're constantly retreating emotionally and leaving me behind? You must take me with you into that darkness."

"Katie"—I backed away—"that's not something I can do."

"You can. Figure it out, Thomas."

"Your mother doesn't approve of us, you know."

"I don't need my mother's approval. I have yours. Remember?"

Her birthday party at the executive mansion. My words. I'd told her how beautiful she was, and she had responded with a remark about not meeting her mother's approval.

I nodded, remembering that night—her loveliness, my first taste inside that pretty mouth.

"And before you say it, no, my father won't assume the same opinion. He's different. You'll see."

"You bought an airline reservation behind my back. I've worked hard to earn your trust from day one. Christ, I've done things I would never do for another woman."

"Listen, Drogo. Maybe punctuate with an interrogative now and then. Because you're really not making a great case for wanting me '*there, here, everywhere*.' In fact, you're grappling with excuses. Though you are right about that one. I should have discussed my Oxford plans and the reservation with you, and I'm sorry.

"But hey, if it helps, my mom took away my credit card." Her high-spirited manner disappeared, and her eyes filled with sorrow. "She doesn't want to speak to me again until I adjust my 'shamelessly defiant conduct,' as she called it."

I stared in disbelief, watching tears rebuild in her eyes and then fall one by one, each like a knife into my chest. Carolyn Reed would pay for hurting Katie. I knew somehow I would also be punished for doing the same.

I gathered Katie into my arms and murmured against her hair, "I'm sorry, baby. She's an arsehole. I'm an arsehole. Forgive me."

The scent of her hair, her skin, the way her body molded perfectly to mine. I was mad for her, and goddamn it, I needed to make things right.

Her head was on my chest, her warm tears soaking

through my shirt. "Forgiving you is becoming a regular thing."

She was right.

"I won't hurt you again, Katie. I promise. Don't worry about money. I'll take care of everything, here and in England."

She lifted her head, her chin. Her cheeks were flushed. "You want me to go?"

I took her face between my hands. "Of course. I want you to be happy."

"Thank you. My mother can keep her money. I don't want it. And I won't take yours either. My fellowship is fully funded and includes a housing stipend. I'll wait tables or serve coffee. When I get on that flight tomorrow, I'll be on my own."

My heartbeat stilled.

I released her, stepped back. "What?"

"I made commitments. The department head asked me to join the summer research team."

A hand through my hair, I paced round the room. Desperation gripped me. There was no way I would lose her. This had to go down on my terms. I would be the one to send her. John couldn't travel so soon. I had to trust Evans to deliver her safely.

"You'll allow me to help. If you want to do battle over it, that's quite all right with me. You will lose this one, Katie." I stopped pacing, needed to touch her. "I'll charter a private jet for you and Evans. He will keep you safe at Will's house. Evans will drive you to Oxford or escort you in the company helicopter. I'll get there as quickly as John is able to travel."

"Thomas," she said, touching my arm. A soft, long sigh. "Please listen. Don't say anything until I'm finished."

I nodded, touched her temple with the back of my fingers.

"Last night, I thought I'd ruined us, that I'd let you down. Today though, after seeing my mother and now with your unwillingness to make me a full partner in this relationship, I see things differently. It's true—John's attack happened because of me. I understand why you blame me. But *we've* ruined us, if there even was an us.

"So, I'm saying all this because I don't want you to come. I want time on my own. I'll stay at your brother's home in London for the summer, but I've been assigned to Balliol College, and I'll stay there during my five course terms."

There it was. What I'd wanted for her all along. Time for her to be free, to be free of me. But she'd changed me, and I'd changed my mind.

"You're leaving to attend Oxford University, but are you also leaving *me*, Katie?"

"I think that I am. You looked at me for so long with guilt in your eyes, as if we'd done something wrong, as if *we* were wrong."

"Katie—"

"No, I know you're working to get past it. I see it. But

here we are, still not a couple, not really. You're stuck inside your own darkness because you won't share it with me. I mean, it's part of the reason I'm so attracted to you. It suits me in many ways. And I wanted to go through it with you."

I nodded. It was my fault. I was losing her because I couldn't get my shit straight. I'd been so afraid of hurting her that I couldn't see my fear was the source of her pain.

"You're quite wrong about John. I don't blame you. He made a mindful decision to be like Will and me, against our wishes. He understands the risks. When I watched you last night with him as he lay there, bleeding, and then later at the hospital, I wasn't experiencing resentment, Katie. It was reverence. And because I'm a selfish prick, I didn't know what to do with it. The truth is, you amazed me."

"But you left me alone. No explanation. I can't read your mind, and the whiplash from this on-and-off thing you do is too painful. So, yeah, please don't follow. Give me some time."

"I owe you as much. Even stronger than that is my desire to give you whatever you need. Do you understand that I'm not letting you go, Katie, that I'm giving you space?"

She didn't respond. She only stared, her eyes on mine.

Taking my wallet from my trousers, I pressed a credit card in the palm of her hand. "There's no limit. Use it. No waiting tables or making coffee. You'll stay at my brother's house in London for now. I'm not asking. You're still in my protective custody, and you'll continue to follow my rules as such."

There was enough fire in my tone for Katie to know not to argue with me. I wasn't a man to back down. No matter how stubborn Katie was, I was formidable.

Katie opened her mouth to complain, but I shut it down with a hard kiss. It was possessive, unrestrained. She fell into it with me, her sweet tongue rubbing against mine.

I broke the kiss and held her gaze. Those innocent eyes. The gray storm that grew inside them.

Breathless, palms against my chest, card still in one hand, she pushed away. We stood like immovable stone for a minute, eyes locked in, her breath slowing. Then, she leaped into my arms, wrapped her long legs round my hips, and smashed her lips against mine.

I couldn't help but smile against her kiss.

I owned her, and no matter how far she ran across the globe, she was mine.

"Leave me for now, little bird. But understand, the separation is temporary."

"You have me today and tonight, Drogo. Better use the time wisely."

twenty-three

THOMAS

Every day of Katie's life had been planned by her parents, her future spread out before her in rational blocks. Specific, measurable, calculated precisely. They hadn't allowed room for her passions or for spontaneity. She'd lived on twenty-five percent of Manhattan Island. Less than six fucking square miles.

I'd broken that goddamn emotional cage.

Katie hit the gallery, wearing a white blouse, distressed skinny jeans, and bright pink heels. She carried a beige handbag in the crook of her elbow. Long blonde hair hung over her shoulders, the ends curling as they fell onto her breasts. Her glossy, plump lips curved, and her smile lit up the space. Lit up my own smile, my heart, my cock.

Every part of me belonged to her.

The lift bell chimed, and I stepped aside, allowing Marta to come into the gallery.

"Marta!" Katie cried, running to her former nanny and housekeeper's embrace.

"I had to say good-bye and wish you luck. I'm so happy for you, sweetheart."

Marta met my eyes over Katie's shoulder. She mouthed the words, *Thank you.*

I nodded.

The two women parted.

"I have missed you. How is Lena? Did she get the summer internship at that fashion house?"

"She did. It's already keeping her terribly busy, which is good. She has been so lost without you, Katherine."

"Same. It's been difficult, but this thing with Dad will be over soon. I'll come back to visit."

I rotated my wrist for the time. Put my hand on Katie's back. "We must go. Marta agreed to stay and help you pack later."

Katie turned to me, gratitude shining in her eyes. I shook my head, warning her not to say *thank you,* and she smiled, giving a small nod.

In the car, I stared at her, recalling the day that I'd gone to find her, imagining how she would look, sitting in the seat next to me. That fantasy hadn't compared to the beautiful, living, breathing, smiling image before me now.

Carl stopped the car, briefly double-parking in front of Jack's. He stepped out and opened Katie's door, smiling at her. "Your coffee awaits, Miss Reed."

She looked back at me before getting out, a grin on her

face. "Did you lock the place down or buy it out or something?"

"Jack assured me the place was quite empty at this time. Go on then, before I change my mind."

Katie popped out with a chuckle. "You're full of surprises today."

I followed, grinning, pulling her hand into mine as we entered the shop. She stopped abruptly after spotting Lena on the leather sofa in the back, talking to Jack.

Tears glistened in her eyes, and her voice broke. "Thomas."

I pointed to a table at the front. "I'll just be here, taking care of some business. Stay within my sight, Katie. We leave in one hour."

I kissed her hand, letting her go, and watched her walk away. A preview of what was to come, the punishment I deserved.

My chest tightened. Agony sliced through me. I pulled in a long, heavy breath through my nostrils and exhaled while clutching the center of my chest.

Carl came inside after he parked the car properly. My second set of eyes. And more. "I don't mind at all. We can get John settled at your apartment first, and then I'll run the two of you back to the penthouse and pick up my wife. Karah and I can stay with your brother until you return tomorrow evening."

My mobile rang with an incoming call from London—the update I was expecting from Jax. Before answering, I gripped Carl's shoulder for a moment. "Thanks, mate."

KATIE DRAGGED HER NAILS THROUGH THE SCRUFF ALONG my jaw, her body imprisoned by mine, pinned against the inside of her bedroom door. "I know you don't want me to say it, but you did tell me that you'd give me everything, so give me this. Because, damn it, I need to express how grateful I feel. You made this day special for me, Thomas." She placed a warm kiss on my lips. "Thank you."

I ran my thumb over her bottom lip. "I don't want you to feel indebted to me, is all. You've already given me far more than I will ever give you."

It was our last night together. I didn't know how long she would make me wait or if she would even take me back once she started her program at Oxford.

She had to take me back. I could no longer live without her.

"Dinner was really"—she gasped and released a little cry as I pulled her head to the side, using a handful of her hair, kissed her throat, tugged her skin between my teeth—"good. So. Good."

I needed her more than I'd ever needed anything. Needed to touch her, taste her, shove inside her, feel her breathy moans on my skin, hear her scream my name. "I can't stop tonight, Katie. Don't even want to try. Tell me that's what you want."

I'd intended only to hold her that night, as I'd done all along, one more chance to explore my feelings for her while she slept in my arms. For some mad reason, I'd thought I could find enough satisfaction in her sleeping breaths, watching her, dreaming about being with her.

"Yes. Oh God, yes." She pushed her hand between our bodies, stroked my erection. "I want you to put this inside me. Please."

I couldn't hold back, couldn't fight the delicious torment of wanting her any longer. Another jerk on her head. I devoured her mouth with mine, thrusting my tongue in and out, showing her what I planned to do with my cock. She moaned and clung to my neck, accepting my rough kiss, making me grow harder still.

I stepped back, unbuttoning my shirt. "Take off your clothing." I wanted to watch. Needed it to slow me down, so I didn't hurt her. "Do it slowly. No touching yourself."

Katie unbuttoned her blouse and made a show of extending her arm and opening her fingers, letting it fall to the floor. She unsnapped the front hook on her bra and did the same with it. Smiling, biting her bottom lip, she took her time with the button and the zipper on her jeans.

My eyes didn't leave her body. I dropped my shirt. Kicked off my shoes. Watching, scarcely tolerating the way this woman teased me. She knew better, knew that she would pay for doing it.

She worked her hips from side to side while pushing down her slim jeans, making me groan. Small, lacy knickers released from one finger onto the pile.

"Turn round."

Silky, long tresses fell down her back, pulling my eyes to her beckoning arse.

She looked back at me, still with the provocative smile, and dragged her fingertips along her hip, to her breasts, and up to her shoulder before dropping her hand.

I moved in behind her, pressed myself against her arse, cupped her breasts, kissed her neck. "You do understand how this works, Katie. You tease; I punish."

"Do it," she breathed. "Fuck me."

I smirked, pushed two fingers inside her, fucking her with my fingers, allowing my thumb to brush against her clit. She moaned and rocked against my hand to increase the touch.

Close to her ear, quite close, I growled, "Fucking you is not the punishment, baby."

She was wet, rocking, close to coming. I withdrew my hand, wrapped my arms round her to prevent any movement.

"Okay. All right," she said, "I'll obey you."

"Good. Now, get on the bed. Open your legs." I released her.

She turned, her cheeks rosy, lifted her chin, kissed me, and then went to the bed. I followed, watched, gripping my arousal as she spread her legs for me, showing me her pretty pink cunt. I took out a condom from my pocket, dropped my trousers. Climbed on to the bed, down on all fours. I kissed her, my mouth moving from her ankle to the inside of her thighs.

Her breath quickened, her chest rising and falling faster as I used my tongue to pleasure her, to make her come, to make her ready for me. Nothing else, no fingers, only my mouth. I wanted her on the edge, not able to step over it, clinging to the anticipation. I wanted her to desperately crave me the way that I craved her. I pulled her clit between my teeth, and she cried out. Again, and then she screamed my name, earning her climax.

Christ, she was beautiful. Responsive to my touch. My entire body shook with need.

In swift frustration, I grabbed the condom and shot up her body, quickly rolling it on. Cuffed her wrists together in one hand, held them above her head. I used my knees to open her legs wider and pressed my erection against her warm seam. She was already wet, but I wanted her wetter and softer before I entered her. My cock was hard and angry. I would tear her, causing her pain.

She moaned and circled her hips, rubbing her clit against the head of my cock. I needed to be inside her. I needed to come inside her sweet heaven. I kissed her fiercely, owning her, my tongue sweeping against hers. The vibration of her whimper rippled through my mouth and down my spine.

"More," she begged, writhing against me. "Please."

Her legs clung to my hips, raising her to just the right position for me to enter her. I pushed into her folds.

"Don't stop," she cried.

"Slowly," I said. "I'm quite big. I need you to be softer for me."

I pushed in farther, grunted. A sharp breath escaped Katie's lips. I kissed them and thrust with my hips, breaching her delicate walls. She let out a small, erotic scream. Tears ran down along her temples. But Christ, she was hot and tight, my own little heaven.

"Breathe with me." I hovered over her mouth, inhaling every breath she exhaled.

Katie's eyes burned into mine, and she watched my weakness with wide wonder. Nodding, she whispered, "I'm ready."

I released her wrists and slid a hand down between us, circling and pressing until she bucked with pleasure and shook from another orgasm.

It was more than I could bear. The wild desire, the clenching of her perfect little heaven round my throbbing hard length. I thrust in deeper. A mad need to chase her orgasm overtook me. Desperate, uncontrollable. I rocked her into the mattress with rhythmic grunting, pressing her down with my weight, bruising her, tearing her, filling her with all of me.

A roar broke from my throat as I exploded into her, pain and joy and pleasure hitting me all at once. I bit down on her shoulder, tasting her sweetness, inhaling her scent.

Then, I collapsed, completely fucking ruined by her, my heart pounding violently against my rib cage. Nothing could have prepared me for the glorious agony it was to love her.

"I'm in love with you, Katie," I heard myself say roughly. In that moment, I was open to her, completely vulnerable.

She didn't respond, not with words. She held on to me, kept her eyes focused on mine. Her tender embrace soothed me, calmed the dark song in my mind, eased my sinful black soul. She was my salvation.

I kissed her tenderly on the forehead and on her temple, rolled onto my back, and pulled her to my chest.

"Did you like it?" she whispered.

"It was everything, baby. There will never be anything lovelier."

Katie had brought me to my goddamn knees.

twenty-four

THOMAS

I'd thought I understood the fierce love my brother Will had for his wife. It was no secret to what lengths he had gone for her. He had endured physical and emotional pain, carrying the weight of her life on his shoulders, watching from a distance, waiting years to have her.

He'd killed for her.

And because he loved her, he'd been denied his child for eight years.

It was the darkest form of love. Obsession. Possession. Control. It was how my father had loved my mother as well.

Katie deserved time to think things through. She knew if she chose me, I would own her. In exchange for my promise to worship her every day for the rest of my life, she would belong to me. Negotiation didn't exist in this kind of commitment. Only a strong, forgiving woman could love a man like me.

I'd moved back into my own flat. There was no reason for me to stay at the Reeds' penthouse. Carolyn had refused to aid me in her husband's matter, and with her daughter gone, our business had ended.

After looking in on John, I poured myself some scotch and settled in the solitude of my living room. I needed downtime to focus. Track down Chris Reed before the assassin found him. The blinds on the floor-to-ceiling windows remained open, the city lights reflecting on the East River. It was a great view, but it meant nothing to me. I needed to get the hell out of New York.

My mobile rang, the number of the penthouse security office on the screen. "What?" I snapped.

"We have a situation," the security officer said. "We've had our eyes on 4-C, like you asked. Someone just came out of the apartment and took the elevator up to the penthouse."

"Description."

"About six feet, fit, wearing jeans and a black hoodie."

"How many men do you have on detail?" I demanded.

"Myself and two other officers. Should we call the police?"

"No. Disable the power to the lift. Do not engage, for fuck's sake. Assume the man is armed and dangerous. I'm on the way. In the meantime, bring in the rest of the team, but remember—and I can't stress this enough—don't do anything until I arrive."

The Reeds' penthouse was a ten-minute ride on my motorbike.

When I arrived, tenants lingered outside on the pavement, annoyed because they hadn't been allowed inside. One of the security guards stood at the lobby entrance door, arms crossed and legs splayed wide to prevent anyone from slipping through.

I pushed my way to him. "Report."

"Nothing new, sir," he said at full attention. "Nobody in or out."

"Are the stairwells secure?"

He shook his head. "We've had some trouble moving some of the tenants. They figured out they could still use the stairwells."

I nodded. "When the other men get here, I want one on every floor."

"Roger that."

He saluted me as I passed through, as if I were his goddamn drill sergeant. Another guard waited by the lift. As instructed, they'd cut the power. I knew the main stairwell stopped below the penthouse. Beyond that, there was a private stairwell with restricted access leading to the penthouse. I'd installed dead bolts and motion sensors on those doors, controlled by my system. None had been breached.

The problem was, I couldn't disable them without my equipment. I'd moved everything to my flat. Powering up the lift was out of the question. Too much risk. The only way in was the fire escape.

I took the stairs two at a time. When I hit the fourth level, I broke into 4-C, kicking in the door. The wood split where it met the frame. Reed needed to address that issue on all units.

I climbed out an east-facing window—just below Katie's bedroom suite terrace—and took the fire escape up to the penthouse level. The terrace was seven feet away from the ladder. I'd taken apart the landing that gave access to her room.

At six-four, I was strong and in my best form, so it wasn't an impossibility for me to make the jump. I calculated the trajectory, took a couple deep breaths, and went for it. I caught the cement railing with my fingers and pulled myself up and onto the terrace.

Grief hit me with the memory of seeing Katie watching the moon from that very spot. How she'd stripped for me just inside the French doors. The scent of her hair still lingered on my shirt, the softness of our last kiss on my mouth. The feel of her warm flesh was still present on my fingertips.

Grief turned to rage at the cold realization it was me who had pushed her away. I couldn't get my shit together enough to hold on to the woman I loved. That same rage propelled me to continue the task already in motion. Cracking a glass pane with my elbow, I reached inside and unlocked the door leading into Katie's bedroom.

With my gun in hand, I planned to work my way through the flat and check every room.

The gallery came into view, as did the back of a man's head.

With my pistol aimed at him, I warned, "Move one fucking inch, and you're a dead man."

The glass in his hand hit the floor, shattering to pieces at his feet. "Please," he begged with his hands up, fingers stretched out in full view. "Please, this is my home."

He wasn't armed, and he was frightened.

Not the assassin. It was Chris Reed.

I holstered my gun. "Turn and face me. Then, you can tell me what the hell you're doing, Reed, sneaking into your own home like a common thief."

He let out an audible rush of breath and turned. "Hastings. Oh Christ, I thought it was the hit man."

"Make no mistake, the prime minister's assassin will come for you. Talk, or you'll get no help from me."

"Yes, yes. Let's go into the library." He poured himself another glass of Macallan and one for me while I rang the security team.

"I want answers, mate, or things could get quite uncomfortable for you. You want me on your side."

He bobbed his head and clutched his glass as if it were his lifeline. "I'll tell you whatever you need to know, but first, I'd like to know where you sent my daughter."

"Katie's safe, and that's all you'll get until I know what

you did to cause the British prime minister to put a price on your head."

His eyes widened. "I'm innocent. I swear. Whatever they think—"

"Listen to me carefully. I don't want to hear vague explanations or bullshit excuses. Your daughter was almost killed. You should know that if a hair on her head had been harmed, we wouldn't be having a conversation right now."

He sighed heavily and sank onto his leather sofa. "Okay. Bear with me. The situation is complicated. It's a long story."

"Cut to the goddamn chase, Reed."

"Well, okay. What it boils down to is my wife's infidelity. She was unfaithful, and her affair produced a child. I've been searching for intel on the boy's whereabouts, not committing espionage."

"Go on."

"Carolyn's son has level three ASD. The prime minister is the boy's father. They fought. He didn't want the boy, but he also didn't want his wife or the public to find out about the child or his affair with my wife. Carolyn hid their son, afraid the prime minister would come for him—or worse, that he would, well, end the boy. The boy's guardian recently betrayed Carolyn by moving the child. We believe the prime minister has their son now. I've been searching for him."

"What benefit did you gain from disappearing?"

"A man known to be collecting information for me

inside the UK was executed. There were texts between us. Nothing criminal. Enough to alarm the minister. I panicked, and Carolyn said hiding was for the best, to keep Katherine safe. I came back against my wife's wishes. I've been here, in the vacant apartment in my building, for the past three days. I *borrowed* my sister's car."

My jaw clenched. I flexed my fists. "The governor was wrong." A swallow of scotch burned the back of my throat. "I presume you have corroborating evidence to back up your story."

"A paternity test was administered early on. The records were buried, but we were able to retain a copy of the report with the results."

He went on to tell me about the countless threats they'd received from the prime minister over the years. He believed Carolyn's intentions were good.

"You've forgiven your wife for her infidelity?"

He shrugged. "I love her."

"Of course." I understood his kind of forgiveness now. "Sit tight while I make some calls. You need to make one of your own—use the landline to ring your daughter. Katie needs to hear from you. Her new number is there, on your desk."

"Hastings, wait. You've used that name several times. Are you personally involved with my daughter?"

I turned my back on him to leave the room. "Make the call. Do it now."

Katie was close to her father. I wanted her to have the opportunity to tell him.

When I returned to the library, Reed was on the leather sofa, another glass of scotch in his hand.

He scrubbed a hand over his face before making eye contact with me. "I'm at a loss. I don't know how to process this relationship between you and Katherine."

My chest split. "She left me, you know."

He nodded, examining my expression, my hand on my chest. "I'm sorry, I think. Yes, I believe that I am. She had no choice but to keep the truth from you. It wasn't her secret to tell."

I went to the bar, built into one of his wooden bookcases, and filled my glass. "Quite right. She's blameless." I took a drink, turned. "The director general demands your cooperation. In return, his team will take out the remaining assassin, and he'll see that a parliamentary commission forms to investigate the prime minister's actions against you. You'll travel to London in my custody and be remanded by MI5 upon our arrival."

Reed opened his mouth, but before he could speak, I cut him off. "Think carefully before you respond, mate. Leaving with me is your only ticket to stay alive and to see your daughter again."

"Okay. Then, I will go. And Carolyn's son?"

"If your wife wants to establish custody of the child properly, she must raise the legal matter in England, where the child resides." I checked my watch. "The director's plane arrives in thirty-six hours. I'll meet you here three hours prior to that. I trust you're not going to run again."

He shook his head. "You have my word. For my family's sake."

The next thing that entered my mind was Katie, the thought that she might refuse to see me.

My hand shook as I set down the glass.

twenty-five

KATIE

THE SOFT SOUNDS OF KENSINGTON AND ITS PICTURE-perfect green spaces resonated in my soul when I stepped outside, leaving the cute coffeehouse/wine bar. I supposed one chose coffee or wine based on the time of day or occasion. The little café was in the center of a garden square. So unlike Manhattan.

The Royal Borough of Kensington called out to the elite with its luxurious boutiques and restaurants, the iconic Royal Albert Hall, and the hushed residential streets, lined with trees and pristine white Victorian homes. Gone were the sirens and honking car horns and concrete jackhammering. It was easy to see why Thomas was indifferent about New York.

I missed him. I couldn't stop thinking about our last day together. He'd surprised me with visits from Marta and

Lena, with his desperate kisses and the way he'd made love to me. My first, my everything. He'd liberated me from my small, detached life. I was a whole person in his eyes, a woman, not a fragile child prodigy. But like a spoiled toddler, I'd still turned him away.

So, there I was, without him, exploring the neighborhood for the first time since I'd arrived in London four days earlier. The first three days had dragged on. I'd met with my college advisor at Balliol, the Mathematical Institute's senior professor, and the lead from my research group, all while experiencing the effects of jet lag.

I couldn't have been happier with my research group assignment. Professor Beam had charged us with targeting the fundamental mathematical aspects of random matrix theory and several associated areas of research, including number theory and quantum chaos.

"New York is three thousand four hundred fifty-six miles away from here," I told my chaperone, Jessica Johnson.

Will had informed Andrew and me at the airport that Jessica would stay with us in London for a while. I'd understood at once and turned my head to hide a smile. Thomas had ordered it. His possessive behavior pleased me, satisfied a deep-rooted obscure need.

Jessica was Ellie's best friend, Will had said. I'd stared at him as he spoke, stared at his familiar eyes.

Thomas was very much the image of his older brother. They shared distinct features. Light-blue eyes, remarkably broad shoulders, the smirky mouth. Will was leaner and had a harder edge. Thomas was intimidating, a man not to be challenged, and his brother gave off even more of the same dangerous vibe.

I couldn't help but imagine how John would change through his twenties and become even more like his brothers, his features hardening, his presence growing darker. I'd spoken to him just after I arrived, and he was doing well.

It's also the distance between Thomas and me, I wanted to add to my response. "Are you finished quizzing me now?"

"Sorry. I'm fascinated," Jessica said. "You're literally a human calculator."

She stopped me, her palms against my shoulders, which brought Andrew Evans to a halt behind us as well.

"Call him, Katie. I can see that you're thinking about him. This family has a dark past, but now, it's filled with love and support and fierce devotion. I know you've seen that in Thomas."

We continued walking.

"I have seen Thomas's generosity and his commitment to family, and I admire him deeply for it. But I can't call him, not yet. I need more time to process everything."

Jessica smiled. "I totally get it. He's an intense guy. Settle into your new routine first."

"We didn't part on bad terms, Jess. He understands me."

"Yeah. His strength is such a huge part of the family's support. He belongs here, not in New York."

Jessica was the type who didn't care if people saw what was in her heart. She spoke lovingly of "the family" often, as if it were her own. I was sure they felt the same way about her. It was easy to be comfortable with her. Maybe it was because she was a nurse by training, skilled in easing the pain and suffering of others.

She was also a gorgeous American, twenty-eight, like Thomas, and a total badass if ever there was one. Scarlett Johansson with long red hair. She wore skinny jeans, cuffed above her ankle boots, and a cropped leather jacket over her hip-length white T-shirt. A dainty silver cross hung from her neck.

Heat abruptly pumped through my blood, my heartbeat sped up, and my hands flexed, as if they wanted to ball into fists. Jealousy was stirring inside me. Another emotion I wasn't used to experiencing.

Andrew's phone rang, startling me. He dropped back a few paces, and he kept his voice low, his tone changed. It was Thomas, checking in on us.

I took a deep breath. "Can I ask you something, Jess?"

"Sure. Ask away."

"Have you been with Thomas? I mean, you're beautiful, and I know you've spent time with him. He wouldn't trust you with my safety otherwise."

"Katie. Really, girl? Do I look like his type?" She shook her head and laughed. "I'm not. Nor is he mine. Thomas is like my brother, and the time we've shared has been in the gym. He helps me with hand-to-hand fight training. I'm actually seeing Ben Scott."

"Oh. I'm so sorry … I shouldn't have assumed."

"It's okay. This family dynamic is different. Friends are the family you choose, right? Ben is Will's best friend. He's the head of security operations, and he helps manage the properties. He and his daughter, Chelsea, also live on the estate. Take my advice: don't doubt Thomas's feelings for you. I get it can be difficult sometimes, but just remember, when one of these men loves you, there's no one and nothing else."

Jessica put her arm around my shoulders, and we shared a knowing laugh. "Now, let's talk about another guy … your brother."

I gasped, stopped walking. "What? How did you—"

"Will called this morning and asked me to have this conversation with you. Thomas found your father. He's quite well, no injuries. Katie, you should know that your father told Thomas everything, and he surrendered into Thomas's custody."

She took my hand. "I want you to hear me when I say your dad is going to be just fine. MI5 is holding him for further questioning while they investigate his claims against the prime minister. The director general will send him home soon, back to his life as it was."

The truth was out. My family would be safe.

I squeezed my lids shut for a moment. The nightmare

was ending, but not because my mother had taken responsibility for what she'd done—for the lies, the heartless way she'd treated my brother, the pain she'd caused us all. I knew my mother, and she would have allowed it to go on until one of us was dead. It was Thomas who had unchained my father and me from the governor's secrets.

I nodded, squeezing Jessica's hand.

"I promise your dad will be okay. Thomas won't let anyone harm him."

A single tear, relief and hope washing through me. "Have they found Hudson?"

The governor had named my younger brother after the damn river. She'd left my father and me when I was six months old. A business trip, she'd told him. A year later, Dad had taken her back.

One year, four months, and two days separated Hudson's birthday from mine. Something other than time and distance also separated us. A gene moderator. I had it, neurologists and psychologists had said, and he didn't. It allowed my gift to shine. Society had labeled me a child prodigy and Hudson an autistic child.

I'd seen him twice, that I could recall, the last time when he was fifteen.

"Thomas is looking for him. The Hastings influence in this country is incredible. It won't take long to get a location." She tugged on my arm, looked over her shoulder at Andrew. "We've been in one area for a while. Shall we head back to the car?"

He nodded with his phone still held close to his ear.

Thomas. God, I owed him more than I'd given. I wanted desperately to rip the phone away from Andrew. I wanted to tell Thomas that I had wanted him to follow me, that I'd been stupid and selfish. To ask for *his* forgiveness. The investigation had been for his brother, but the man he'd killed was for me. He had tolerated the governor and been easy on my father. Now, he was searching for my brother.

All or nothing. In the end, he'd chosen all. For me, for us.

It was time for me to do the same.

FIFTEEN MINUTES LATER, ANDREW PASSED THROUGH THE security gate and parked in a space inside the private lot beside the house. I yawned, lulled by the brief car ride, and then stepped out. I had slept so little since landing in England.

He entered the code on the electronic security pad and then pushed open the door while extending his arm in front of me, so I couldn't go inside. With a small nod, he sent Jessica into the house alone.

My heart raced. It wasn't how we'd been doing things.

I panicked. "What is it? What's happening?"

Andrew shrugged. "I've been fired. You're no longer in my custody."

"What?"

"Katie," a voice behind me called out.

The hairs on my arm stood on end. Faster and faster, my heart pounded.

His voice. It couldn't be. It had to be. I'd missed something. My bag slipped to the ground. Slowly, I turned. It was him.

It was Thomas.

I couldn't compose a thought, couldn't push words out of my mouth. I could only run. I ran to him, crossing the length of the concrete courtyard between us. He did the same, and we met in the middle. I leaped, knowing he would catch me, hold me in his arms, never let me go again.

Thomas smashed his lips against mine and spun us. I clung to his body with mine. To his heart with mine. We were the sun, and Earth revolved around us. He parted my lips with his tongue and led us into a fierce, deep kiss. We broke, me breathless, him smiling.

"Ride with me, Katie."

Those words … the same he'd said on the day we spent at the park. The day we'd been free. Free from the pain, the guilt. Free to fall in love.

I didn't have any words yet. When they came, they would break me. Tears fell, breaking me anyway. Remorse and relief and happiness rolled down my cheeks, dropping onto his face, his chest. I slid down the front of his body to my feet, still clinging to his neck, and I nodded.

"Close your eyes, little bird."

I closed them, and he kissed each lid tenderly.

"Don't open. Don't move. Feel me, feel us." He waited several seconds, moved his mouth to my ear, and growled, "I will not let you go again. I'll give you anything else—you name it—but not that."

I nodded again with my eyes still shut. I let my head fall back, and I laughed. When I opened to see him, he was grinning. Then, he gripped the back of my head, pulled my mouth to his, and kissed me again. Hard. His bruising kiss, his erection.

I wanted more. I wanted everything he had. His devotion, his generosity, his powerful, possessive kind of love. His body. The darkness that unsettled him.

His lips moved to my neck, kissing, sucking. A soft growl at my ear. "Tell me you understand how fucking desperately I love you. Say the words."

To catch my breath, to gather my thoughts, I pulled back, meeting his white-hot gaze. Seconds passed, an eternity, but still, he waited.

"I won't apologize because you don't want that. I'll make you a promise instead. I won't leave you again. Because I do understand and I love you that way too." I put a soft kiss on his lips.

He pulled my chin higher with his thumb and forefinger. "I won't hold you back. You have my word. I'm buying us a house here, in London. You'll always have a home to come back to, Katie."

"You're my home," I whispered. "I'm ready for that ride, now."

We rode off on his motorcycle, free once again.

There was no roadmap for our future.

Neither of us cared.

We were in love, and that was everything.

coming soon

Thank you for reading *Two Pretty Lies.*

Thomas and Katie's story isn't quite over! An extended epilogue is on the way. Sign up to receive your free copy on the day it releases at www.klclare.com/subscribe.

In case you missed it, the Hastings Brothers series began in the Twisted Beautiful Lies duet. *Twisted Beautiful Lies* and *Her Lovely Lies* are available from your favorite bookseller or www.klclare.com.

Get ready for another irresistible antihero…

In Kelleigh Clare's upcoming Savage Syndicate trilogy, Stefano Rivelli is a notorious mafia boss who takes what he wants, including the woman he once let go—even if having her again means war. Sign up to get release updates at www.klclare.com/subscribe.

about kelleigh clare

Ms. Clare is an award-winning, *USA Today* bestselling author. Before writing contemporary fiction, she was a human resources executive and a progressive voice on women's issues with a global coalition of bloggers. She also contributed to the successful startup of a *Forbes* and *TIME* recognized digital publication for women.

Sign up for news and bonus content at
www.klclare.com/subscribe.

Follow @kelleighclare

CPSIA information can be obtained
at www.ICGtesting.com
Printed in the USA
LVHW100428140422
716131LV00001B/57

9 781735 557533